THE
WILD

THE WILD

OWEN LAUKKANEN

Underlined

Text copyright © 2020 by Owen Laukkanen
Cover art used under license from Shutterstock.com and Unsplash.com

Visit us on the Web! GetUnderlined.com

Educators and librarians, for a variety of teaching tools, visit us at
RHTeachersLibrarians.com

Library of Congress Cataloging-in-Publication Data
Names: Laukkanen, Owen, author.
Title: The wild / Owen Laukkanen.
Description: New York : Delacorte Press, 2020. I Summary: Seventeen-year-old
Dawn and a group of other teens must survive a "wilderness therapy" camp
in Washington State as things quickly and drastically go wrong. I
Audience: Ages 14 and up. (provided by Delacorte Press.)
Identifiers: LCCN 2019045283 (print) I LCCN 2019045284 (ebook) I
ISBN 978-0-593-17975-8 (ebook) I ISBN 978-0-593-17974-1 (trade paperback)
Subjects: I CYAC: Adventure therapy—Fiction. I Survival—Fiction. I
Camping—Fiction. I Murder—Fiction.
Classification: LCC PZ77.1.L379 (ebook) I LCC PZ77.1.L379 Wil 2020 (print) I
DDC [Fic]—dc23

Printed in the United States of America
10 9 8 7 6 5 4 3 2 1
First Underlined Edition 2020

Random House Children's Books supports the First Amendment
and celebrates the right to read.

To Jay and Uncle Darren, who are always
down for a wilderness misadventure

1.

THIS IS THE STORY of a messed-up girl and how her family paid people to send her into the wilderness with a bunch of other messed-up kids in hopes it would somehow make them less messed up.

This is a real thing that happens.

It might even be an eventuality your parents have considered for *you*.

But this is the story of what happens when things

go

wrong.

2.

MEET DAWN. Dawn is the aforementioned messed-up girl. She'll be the protagonist and de facto audience surrogate for this little misadventure.

Dawn is seventeen years old and mostly normal. She lives in Sacramento with a drug dealer named Julian, who is roughly twice her age.

This is a continued point of contention between Dawn and her mother, Wendy. Wendy would prefer that Dawn *not* live with a drug dealer. She'd prefer that Dawn, you know, go to school and not just get high all the time and sneak into clubs.

She'd prefer that Dawn be at home, where Wendy and Dawn's younger brother, Bryce, live with Dawn's stepdad, Cam.

Dawn loves her brother.

She mostly loves her mom.

Dawn does not love Cam. Dawn resents Cam and hates that her mother fell in love with him. Her father's only been gone for two years, and it's too soon to be talking replacements.

Dawn can't stand to be near Cam. It makes her feel like she's betraying her dad. It drives her insane that nobody else sees it that way. That her mother could move on so quickly.

That's why she's staying with Julian.

And that's why she spends her days mostly wasted.

3.

THE CAM/WENDY/DAWN THING has been an ongoing saga. You don't need to know the gory details, but suffice it to say, it's been a lot of screaming and hurt feelings.

It's been a lot of self-medicating and not going to class.

It's been a lot of *Julian*.

Cam and Wendy have been trying to get Dawn to come home. Go to school. Be high less. See less Julian. Be more normal.

Cam and Wendy have failed miserably so far.

But Cam and Wendy have one more bullet to fire.

It's their last resort.

And it's going to *royally* fuck up Dawn's day.

4.

WHAT IT IS, is a straight-up kidnapping.

Cam and Wendy show up at Julian's place at sunset. Dawn and Julian are on Julian's couch, watching cartoons but not really, when Cam knocks on the door. Dawn is too high to get off the couch; she lets Julian answer, hears the door open, hears voices:

Julian, someone else, Julian again.

Then Julian's back, scratching his head and not looking at Dawn.

"It's your stepdad," Julian says. "He says if you don't go talk to him, he's calling the cops."

From the way Cam's face twitches when he sees her, Dawn knows she must look like shit. She hasn't showered since whenever, her hair's a disaster, she's wearing one of Julian's Lords of Gastown T-shirts like a dress.

"What do you want?" she asks her stepdad. Looks past him and sees Wendy standing by the minivan, arms folded across her chest, looking anywhere but at the house.

(Dawn briefly wonders where Bryce is, then decides she's

5

glad he isn't here. She doesn't love the thought of her little brother seeing her like this.)

Cam sets his jaw like he's been rehearsing this moment. He probably has.

(He's probably not a bad guy, Cam. I mean, it's not *his* fault that Dawn's dad is dead. Cam's an accountant, and mostly harmless, and Dawn might actually like him if he were, you know, her *teacher* or something and not someone who acted like he was entitled to any authority over her whatsoever.)

"I need you to come with us, Dawn," Cam says. "It's time to go."

Dawn rolls her eyes, like she always does when Cam starts down this road. "I'm not going anywhere with you, Cam," she tells him. "And you can't make me."

Cam stares at her. Mouth opening and closing like whatever he rehearsed, it didn't get this far.

Then Julian shows up behind Dawn. "I think you should go," he tells her.

Dawn spins, like *WTF?* Julian shrugs. Cam's looking at Julian like he wants to punch him, but he won't—

(Julian's twice his size).

Cam just nods instead, like *Listen to the man.* "Nobody wants the police involved, Dawn," he says.

Cam has a point. Julian knows this.

Dawn knows it, too.

If the police show up, they'll find Julian's stash of pills. They'll find Julian, and they'll find Dawn.

Julian doesn't want any part of this, obviously.

So Julian's turned traitor.

Julian's practically shoving Dawn out the front door.

Go with your parents, Dawn.

GTFO.

So Dawn doesn't put up too much of a fuss. This has happened before. She's thinking Cam and Wendy will pile her into that minivan and just take her home, like they always do.

She's thinking this is just another bullshit power move by Cam to prove he's cut out to be her father, and she'll endure it for a couple of days on the absolute outside and then she'll sneak off again and do what she wants.

And this time she'll make sure Cam and Wendy can't find her.

This is what Dawn is thinking.

It's what she's expecting.

But Dawn is wrong.

Cam takes her to the airport.

5.

"THERE'S NO FUCKING WAY this is legal."

In the airplane seat beside Dawn, Wendy says nothing. She hasn't said much the whole plane ride, won't even answer Dawn's questions.

(Like, why are we on a plane?)

(Why isn't Cam coming?)

(Why did you pack me a bag?)

She's trying so hard to look tough, Dawn can tell. Play the authority figure, the mean mom, but Wendy isn't cut out for that role. She's too *nice*.

But she's trying to be tough, and it's clearly taking work, and watching her, it kind of breaks Dawn's heart a little bit.

(Like, whatever is happening, *you* made her do this.)

(*You* made her this way.)

Dawn would never admit it, but maybe that's why she isn't putting up more of a fuss. Maybe that's why she didn't go bat-shit and scream *kidnapping* when Cam dropped them off at the airport. Because for whatever reason, she didn't.

She put on the shorts Wendy fished out of her overnight

bag, watched Cam hug Wendy goodbye and drive off, and then she followed her mom into the airport and onto the plane and stared out the window and waited to land.

And now they're at the Seattle airport, and it's nighttime and there's a guy standing at the baggage carousel holding a sign with Wendy's name on it. He's around forty, tanned, wearing a blue fleece jacket with the words OUT OF THE WILD on it.

He shakes Wendy's hand.

He doesn't shake Dawn's.

"Come on," he says. "I'm parked in the lot."

6.

THE FLEECE GUY'S NAME IS STEVE. He has a white van with the same words as his jacket written on the side.

OUT OF THE WILD.

Steve throws Dawn's bag in the back of the van. Then he turns back to Wendy. "This usually takes about two to three months," he tells her. "Depending on the kid. You need a ride to your hotel?"

Wendy shakes her head. Says something about a shuttle bus.

"Okay." Steve shakes her hand again. "We'll be in touch."

Dawn's wondering if she's still high or just half-asleep. Can't process what's happening. Then Wendy's hugging her. Telling her she loves her.

She can't look Dawn in the eyes.

Then Wendy's walking away and Steve's opening the passenger door of the van and he's gesturing to Dawn to get in.

"It's just you and me, kid," he tells Dawn. "Your mom ain't coming back."

Dawn doesn't run.

She *thinks* about running, but where would she go? She's

in *Seattle*, for God's sake. And even her mom wants nothing to do with her.

Anyway, Dawn's maybe a little bit curious. So far, nobody's told her shit.

She gets in the van with Steve.

It's a mistake.

7.

STEVE PLAYS THE RADIO while he's driving. Something old and annoying. He drives for a long time, out of the city and into dark countryside. The road winds and climbs into foothills and mountains. Steve doesn't stop at any stop signs for Dawn to jump out. He doesn't pull over for gas or so she can pee.

"Where are you taking me?" Dawn asks him.

Steve glances across at her. He's whistling along with the music, and it's annoying as fuck. "You'll see when we get there," he tells her. He doesn't elaborate.

They drive for a long time. Eventually, they stop.

There turns out to be a couple of ugly little buildings at the end of a long gravel road. There's a bright-yellow light on a pole between them, a dimmer light on in a window. A sign by the window reads PARENTS THIS WAY.

Steve parks the van. Turns it off. Climbs out and walks around to Dawn's door and waits as she climbs out and looks around. "Come on," he tells her, starting toward the building with the light on in the window.

Dawn doesn't follow. She's still looking around. Peering into the darkness at the edge of the light, wondering what would happen if she ran, like, now.

Steve reads her mind. "We'd get you back," he tells her. "Or we wouldn't. And believe me, you'd wish we did."

He gestures to the building again. "Come on."

Dawn follows him.

8.

"GOT A NEW BEAR CUB for you, Tanya."

There's a woman in the building, sitting at a desk behind an old computer monitor. She's younger than Steve. Her hair's pulled up underneath a baseball cap. The cap says OUT OF THE WILD, too. Just like Steve's jacket.

Just like the van.

Tanya stands as Dawn enters the room. She gives Dawn a look, head to toe. "Okay," she says, apparently satisfied. "Come with me."

Dawn glances back at Steve, but he's over at the desk pretending to ignore her. So Dawn follows Tanya deeper into the building. Into an empty room, a bright-white light, no windows. A table and two chairs. A pile of junk in one corner, straps and rope and what looks like a tarp. Dawn stares at the pile of junk. When she looks back, Tanya's snapping on rubber gloves.

(What the fuck?)

"Welcome to Out of the Wild," Tanya says. "We're America's number one wilderness therapy program for troubled

14

youth. Your parents signed you up because they think we can help you."

(What the fuck?)

"From this moment on, you're one of our Bear Cubs," Tanya continues. "You'll remain in the program until you reach Grizzly status. You'll work hard for that status. You'll learn responsibility and respect. You'll learn how to survive in the wild."

"Okay," Dawn says. "What in the actual *fuck*."

Tanya ditches the spiel. Looks Dawn in the eye. "You're here because people care about you, Dawn, and because our program works. By the time you walk out of here, you'll be a whole different person."

Dawn wants to slap her. This feels like a dream. "You're completely nuts," she tells Tanya, "if you think I'm doing any of this. Those people who supposedly care about me? They're the reason I'm so fucked up in the first place.

"I want to go home," she says.

But Tanya is unfazed. "You'll go home when you graduate," she tells Dawn. "Not a minute before. Believe me, it's easier if you just accept it."

She checks her rubber gloves.

"Nothing from the outside world is allowed past this point," she says. "Strip."

What happens next is too demeaning to talk about. Suffice it to say, Dawn walks out of that shitty little room without the clothes she walked in with, without her phone, and with Tanya satisfied she's not holding any of Julian's stash.

"Bear Cubs wear yellow," Tanya tells Dawn, handing her a

pair of cargo pants and a yellow T-shirt. "So we can find you better if you lose the rest of the Pack."

"What the hell is the Pack?" Dawn asks. "Where are you taking me?"

"You'll figure it all out soon enough," Tanya replies. Then she gestures to the pile of junk in the corner. "That's the rest of your supplies. We leave it to you to figure out how to transport it."

Dawn stares at the pile of junk. Can't really make sense of it.

"I'll be back in ten minutes to take you to camp," Tanya tells her. "Good luck."

9.

THE CONTENTS OF DAWN'S PILE OF JUNK:

1. Tarp
2. Wool blanket (scratchy)
3. Parachute cord (20 feet)
4. Assorted straps
5. Sleeping bag
6. Sleeping pad
7. Underwear, two pairs (ugly)
8. Socks, two pairs
9. Yellow T-shirt
10. Yellow fleece
11. Rain shell
12. Waterproof pants
13. Matches
14. Cup
15. Bowl
16. Spork
17. Rice (1 bag)

18. Lentils (1 bag)
19. Raisins (1 bag)
20. Oats (1 bag)
21. Toothbrush
22. Toilet paper (1 roll)
23. Book: *Wilderness Survival*
24. Book: *Don't Get Eaten*
25. Book: *Out of the Wild Rules and Regulations*

"You have to earn your camping backpack," Tanya says, as Dawn staggers out of the building under the weight of her allotment of junk.

(She's tied it all together with the parachute cord and the straps, but things keep falling out every couple of steps. Tanya doesn't offer to help.)

"Easiest way to earn stuff?" Tanya continues, leading Dawn back toward the white van. "Study the rule book. Memorize it. And don't be a shit."

10.

"AND *THAT* IS HOW I WOUND UP in this hellhole."

Four days after the kidnapping and Dawn is still in that banana-yellow Bear Cub bullshit T-shirt, still dropping things from her tarp literally every time she moves. She's still kind of half wondering if this whole fiasco isn't just a bad dream or a bad trip and she's about to wake up in a pool of her own drool on Julian's couch again.

Right now, Dawn is sitting balanced on a lumpy-ass log beside an anemic little campfire, slowly starving to death with the rest of the, quote, unquote, Bear Pack while they wait for the counselors to finish checking the tents before lights-out.

Dawn still doesn't have a tent. She hasn't earned one yet, so she has to rig her tarp into a little lean-to and spread her sleeping bag out underneath it. But she's really not good at the whole "rigging shit up" thing, so half the time she wakes up in the morning with a face full of dirty tarp, and the other half she wakes up freezing cold and damp to find her tarp's blown off into the bushes somewhere. It's September and Washington

State in the mountains is a lot colder than Sacramento and when Dawn's not starving she's pretty well freezing to death.

———

There are six other kids in the group. Four guys and two girls. They span a range of ages and demographics, but mostly they all just look miserable.

Sullen.

Angry.

Tired.

Nobody talks very much in the group because there isn't much time and nobody has any energy. They've been hiking since Dawn got here and maybe since forever, through a never-ending rain forest and over literal mountains. It's too cold most of the time and too hot the rest, and there are weird bugs and spiders and probably cougars and bears, and Dawn's back hurts from the way the rope around her tarp digs into her back when she's trying to carry all of her shit, and she's hungry because all she's eaten is rice and raisins and lentils—

(some of the other kids have, like, energy bars and dehydrated meals and even chocolate, but Dawn has surmised you have to earn that stuff, too)

—and her leg muscles are screaming from having to hike so much, and she twisted her ankle on a tree root somewhere, and she's dirty and smelly and sick of peeing in the woods and having to wear the same underwear every day, but according to one of the guys in the group, Lucas, this is about as good as Out of the Wild gets.

"It's wilderness therapy," Lucas tells her. "Like, you've heard of boot camp and stuff, right? Send all the bad kids to army school and get some drill sergeant to scare the bad right out of them? This is the same shit, but we're mobile." He gestures in the vague direction of the counselors. "And those two dumbasses would make terrible drill sergeants."

The scheme, Lucas explains, is you hike around in the woods more or less nonstop, graduating through the ranks from Bear Cub all the way up to Grizzly, at which point they let you go home.

"It usually takes two or three months, sometimes longer," he says. "I never heard of anyone getting out quicker."

Lucas is wearing a red shirt. That apparently makes him a Black Bear, though why the Black Bears wear red is beyond Dawn's comprehension, until she looks around and notices how every kid in the Pack wears a bright color, no matter what level they are. The Brown Bears wear orange.

"It's because of the forest," Lucas says. "Bright colors make it easier to find you if you escape."

"Or find your body if you die," a girl named Kyla says, rolling her eyes.

Kyla's a Polar Bear. Polar Bears wear blue.

Black Bears are apparently two levels up from Bear Cubs. Brown Bears are between Bear Cubs and Black Bears, and Polar Bears are one level higher than Black Bears. Then it's Grizzly Bears, who wear whatever they want, because that's when you graduate. Lucas has been here for almost a month, so he's doing okay.

Kyla has been here for three months. She's not doing as great.

"They can bust you back down, too," she tells Dawn. "Like, I lost a bag of rice a while back and we had to cut the hike short, so they demoted me to Black Bear again, not like I gave a shit. What I got waiting for me back home? A little walk in the woods is easy."

Kyla's here because she stabbed her mom's boyfriend in the neck with a pen when he tried to put his hands on her, and the judge gave her a choice, jail or this.

"White people are so fucked up," she says. "Like, this is your idea of punishment, you know? Walking. In nature. Rocks and trees and shit. Shit, I should get y'all's parents to pay me to take you through my city, try to survive a week where I'm from. You can even wear your pretty yellow shirt."

Regardless, Kyla has a tent and nice new hiking backpack. She has better hiking boots than Dawn does, and a thicker rain jacket, too.

Polar Bears earn.

So far it hasn't rained, but it's Washington State in September. From what Dawn's heard people saying, it'll start to rain soon, and it won't stop until May. *Awesome.*

There's one other Polar Bear in the Pack, a tall, brooding guy named Warden. There are two Brown Bears and one other Black Bear.

The other Black Bear's name is Brielle, and she doesn't talk much or make eye contact with anyone, but she's a good hiker. She's always up near the front of the Pack.

Dawn's always near the back, always out of breath, always sweating through her yellow shirt and praying for another water break.

The Brown Bears are two guys named Evan and Brandon. They hike together and set their tents up beside each other, and whenever the counselors aren't paying attention, they crack jokes and play fight and generally cause mayhem. They're both medium tall and kind of plain-featured and entirely unremarkable, and Dawn has already confused their names at least once a day since she arrived. They don't say much to her, but sometimes she'll go for water or to find firewood or something and look back and catch their eyes and know they're talking about her and it's kind of creepy. She sets her tarp up far away and generally tries to avoid them.

Lucas, Kyla, Brielle. Warden, Evan, Brandon. Those are the kids in Dawn's, quote, unquote, Pack, and that's about as much as she knows about each of them, at this point in time. They're all messed up, clearly, or they wouldn't be here. They all did something bad enough to get them exiled to this patch of lonely rain forest, anyway. But just who they are and what exactly they're capable of, Dawn's going to have to wait and find out.

And she will.

11.

THERE ARE TWO COUNSELORS shepherding the Bear Pack through the wilderness. The guy counselor is named Christian and he's tall as God and twice as skinny. He's probably around thirty and he looks like a Halloween prop and sounds pretty scary, too, with his deep-ass voice. I know you're not supposed to judge people on their looks, but Christian is ugly, and even more so because he's mean.

According to Kyla, Christian is the one who busted her back down to Black Bear over the rice incident. And also according to Kyla, it wasn't just the rice that got her demoted but also how Christian wants to keep her in the Pack as long as he can because he has a creepy thing for her, and Dawn isn't sure if this is true or not, but Christian *does* spend a lot of time looking at Kyla and making weird comments that are probably inappropriate about how she looks and what she's wearing and other stuff of that nature.

It's not out of the realm of possibility that Christian's a weirdo, is what I'm saying.

The other counselor is a woman named Amber—because they're *always* named Amber—and she's younger than Christian, and shorter and nicer to look at. She's not as mean, either. Lucas says she has a degree in young adult development or something, which is better than Christian, who probably did his doctorate in How to Be an Asshole.

Amber isn't mean, but she's pretty stern. She doesn't take any shit, like when Dawn's dragging ass at the back of the Pack near the end of the day, Amber will come back there and not necessarily yell but certainly convey with words and tone the urgency of Dawn not, you know, sucking so much. Amber's the one who makes sure everyone gets their chores done in the morning and is packed up and ready to move out while Christian sometimes sleeps in and sometimes just sits around the fire drinking his coffee and "supervising."

Evan and Brandon sometimes talk back to Amber, and Warden and Kyla mostly ignore her, but Dawn does what she says, and so do Lucas and Brielle, though Dawn isn't sure if this is because she/they actually respect Amber or just because they don't want to get Christian involved.

Anyway, those are the counselors. Christian is a dick, and Amber's good at her job. And at least one of them is going to die.

12.

BEFORE THE DYING AND STUFF HAPPENS, though, I'd better tell you a little more about what life is like for the Bear Pack, day to day, so you can bond with these characters and make attachments and know who you're supposed to root for when it all goes to shit.

Like right now, for instance, our motley collection of bad apples is arranged around their sickly campfire, dreaming about Burger King Whoppers and burritos and extralarge double-cheese pizzas as darkness falls and Amber and Christian check on the tents before lights-out.

Dawn is retelling her Origin Story: how her mom and her stepdad jacked her out of Julian's house and kidnapped her and brought her up here, and Lucas and Kyla are listening and nodding, and even Brielle looks like she wants to contribute to the discussion, but she can't, because just as she opens her mouth, Christian shows up out of the gloom across the fire and fixes his creepy eyes on Dawn.

"Bear Cub," he says. "Your shelter sucks. Fix it."

And everyone looks at Dawn, and Dawn inwardly groans

and after a second she stands and circles the fire and follows Christian into the darkness, trying not to think about the way he looks at Kyla and hoping he won't start looking at her the same way.

He doesn't do anything weird, though, just leads Dawn through the bushes to Amber, who's standing where Dawn strung up her bright-orange parachute cord between two saplings and draped her tarp over the top of it. It's kind of windy tonight, and Dawn put rocks on each corner of the tarp to hold it steady, but the rocks didn't work and now the tarp's half blown away, and Amber's standing there shining her flashlight on Dawn's sleeping bag and the rest of her collection of stuff.

"Not good enough, Dawn," Amber says, and in the dim light Dawn can see that Amber's shaking her head, her mouth set in a thin line. "Rain's supposed to start next week, and if you want to stay dry, you're going to have to learn to make better shelter."

Dawn stares at Amber, then down at her not-good-enough tarp. "Everyone else gets a tent," she says. "This wouldn't even be an issue if you'd just give me a tent like the rest of the Pack."

Christian kind of snort-laughs behind her. "Gotta earn your tent," he says, turning to leave.

Amber and Dawn watch him go. Then Amber turns back to Dawn and her expression softens. "Keep working at it," she tells Dawn. "If you can tough it out with the tarp for a good solid week, we'll get you a tent next time we resupply, okay?"

Dawn rolls her eyes. "What about a flashlight?" she asks, because Amber is leaving and taking the flashlight with her, leaving Dawn to tough it out with the tarp in the dark. "Can I have a little light, at least?"

Christian laughs again, from somewhere in the dark. "Gotta earn that, too," he says, and then he and Amber are gone, and Dawn's feeling around for her tarp like a blind person, wondering how she's supposed to earn anything if they won't let her see the way.

Dawn struggles with her tarp and it's shitty and frustrating. She gets dirt all over her sleeping bag and the rest of her stuff, and she scratches her hands and her arms feeling around for bigger rocks in the bushes to hold the tarp down. It's almost completely dark now, and she can hear Christian and Amber telling the rest of the Pack it's time for lights-out. Dawn can't find any big rocks, and her tarp's flapping all over the place—

> (and she's just about to give up and sleep out in the open and hope Amber doesn't notice and it doesn't rain in the night)

—when something rustles beside her and Dawn nearly screams in terror, thinking it's a cougar—or worse, Christian—but then that something whispers her name and tells her to be quiet and it's actually Lucas, and he holds his flashlight up to his face and gives her a goofy grin so that she knows it's him.

"I thought you could maybe use a little help with that tarp," Lucas says.

13.

"I DIDN'T ACTUALLY DO ANYTHING WRONG," Lucas tells Dawn as he helps her retrieve her tarp from the tangle of bushes where it's been blown by the wind. "My dad signed me up for this because he thought it would be good practice for the army."

Dawn stares at him, squinting in the glare of his flashlight. "Wait, what? You don't, like, *have* to be here?"

"Oh, I have to be here," Lucas says, laughing. "You never met my dad. He didn't exactly give me a choice."

"Yeah, but." Dawn looks back toward the ring of tents, barely visible in the flickering firelight. "You're not here because you're bad, or whatever. You're not, like, a criminal."

Lucas laughs again. "Are you?"

Dawn hesitates. She's not *technically* a criminal; at least, she's never been arrested. But she's not really a LAW-ABIDING CITIZEN, either. She doesn't want to make any confessions to Lucas, not now that she's heard *his* story.

Lucas reads her nonanswer for the answer it really is, though.

"You don't have to be ashamed or anything," he tells Dawn. "We're freaking teenagers. Nobody's perfect."

It sounds funny, coming out of Lucas's mouth. He's kind of got a golden-boy thing going on, always friendly and helpful and usually pretty happy, like a Labrador retriever or something, with his tousled blond hair and blue eyes and easy smile. He might not be perfect, but he's a lot more perfect than Dawn, anyway. She wonders what Lucas would think if she told him she was sleeping with a thirty-something drug dealer. Wonders if he'd still look at her the same.

She shakes her head clear. Reaches for the tarp, pulls it out of the bushes. "Help me with this," she tells Lucas. "Before Amber and the ghoul come back and see us."

They get the tarp repositioned and mostly pinned down, and then Lucas reaches into his pocket and pulls out something metallic that jingles.

"Tent pegs," he says, grinning, shining his light down so Dawn can see. "Mine came with eight, but I really only need four. You might find they work better than those rocks you've been using."

Dawn looks at them. Four brand-new pegs; they'll fit perfectly in the little holes in each corner of her tarp. "Won't the counselors be mad?" she asks.

Lucas shrugs. "Probably," he says. "Just hide them under those rocks and make sure you take them out in the morning before Amber comes around to check on you. You'll probably get your tent in a few days anyway."

"I hope so," Dawn says. "It's supposed to start raining soon, right?"

"Inevitably." Lucas holds out the pegs. "So don't get caught."

A gust of wind takes hold of Dawn's tarp again, pulls it out from under the rocks and sends one end flapping wildly in the breeze.

"*Shit.*" Dawn jumps up, grabs the tarp, and pulls it back down again. Realizes the stupid rocks aren't ever going to work.

Lucas helps her tamp the tarp down. Holds out the pegs again, smiling that golden-boy smile of his.

"Thanks," Dawn tells him, and when she takes the pegs from his hands, she can feel the warmth of his body, and it lingers on her skin longer than she'd care to admit.

14.

AN AVERAGE OUT OF THE WILD DAY goes something like this:

Wake up at sunrise. Morning chores (clothes, personal hygiene, pump water, build a fire, cook breakfast). Eat breakfast (never enough food). Pack up. Hike. Water break. Hike. Lunch (still not enough). Pump water. Hike. Water break. Hike. Make camp. Evening chores (set up tents/tarp, find firewood, build fire, cook dinner—you guessed it—pump water, tidy dinner stuff, personal hygiene, hang food). Lights-out. Lie under tarp listening for wild animals and trying not to think about how hungry you are.

Sleep, eventually, maybe.

Rinse.

Repeat.

They have to hang all of the food and their toiletries overnight from the tallest tree they can find, which is always a huge pain in the ass, but otherwise the bears will be drawn to the campsite and might even get into your tent/tarp.

Christian has a knife, and Amber has a bear spray canister,

32

and Evan and Brandon have this rumor going that Christian even has a gun somewhere, which Dawn can't really fathom but kind of hopes is true, given how the Bear Pack is, like, marooned in the middle of nowhere, miles from any civilization and close to all sorts of scary wildlife.

(She's only seen one bear so far—one *real* bear—but it was far away down in a grassy meadow, and besides, Amber said it was a black bear and probably just as scared of humans as humans were of it.)

Christian and Amber are supposed to have a radio, too, and an emergency beacon so that if something goes terribly wrong they can contact the home base and alert the proper authorities. According to Lucas, Out of the Wild leases a thousand square miles of terrain that they use for these programs, and it all backs onto some national park, which is like another million acres of mountains and forest and nothingness.

"So if we get lost or go the wrong way, we'll probably die," he says, cheerfully.

Dawn rolls her eyes, but it's actually pretty scary. They've been hiking for five days now, and she hasn't seen another human being besides the other kids in the group. She hasn't even seen any sign of humanity besides the occasional piece of fluorescent flagging tape stuck to a tree to tell the counselors where the trail's supposed to go, and the occasional jet trail from an airplane high in the sky, a reminder that life's going on, somewhere, far from this forest.

Dawn wonders if anyone misses her.

She wonders if it matters.

According to Kyla, who's been here the longest, Out of the Wild has seven or eight different trails through the backcountry that they use to keep Bear Packs moving.

"Each one takes six days," Kyla tells Dawn. "It's like a big circle. We go out for six days and then we come back and get more food and supplies and go out again. Over and over, until you go insane or you graduate."

"Whichever comes first," Lucas says.

They don't know if there are other Bear Packs, or if they're the only one. No one's ever seen another person out here, so they must keep the groups far apart, if there are other groups. Christian and Amber won't say.

"You've been here for, like, months," Dawn tells Kyla. "If there's only seven trails, you must have done this one before, right? Do you recognize it?"

Kyla gives Dawn a look, like *Oh, sweetie.*

"I recognize *rocks* and these big-ass trees," she says. "And the back of Christian's stupid-ass head. Otherwise, I keep my eyes on the ground.

"I don't know where we are, and neither do you," Kyla says. "And neither does Lucas or anyone else. We're totally lost." Kyla blinks at her. "And that's exactly how those asshole counselors like it."

15.

TOTALLY LOST.

Kyla is right. Dawn's been hiking for nearly a week now, and if the rest of the Pack dropped off the face of the earth right this instant, she'd be dead within days, if not hours.

Christian has a map and a compass and the radio—but Dawn's from freaking Sacramento. *Suburban* Sacramento. She isn't exactly proficient with a compass. And anyway, all the rocks and trees look identical.

(That's not totally true. Sometimes the Pack hikes through the rain forest, which is damp and dark and smelly and choked with ferns and bare roots to trip you and big towering trees with branches that claw at your face and your clothes and rip things from your shitty tarp knapsack as you pass. And sometimes they climb up so high onto ridges that they're out of the big trees and it's mostly just stunted, runty evergreens and a lot of bare rock, and you can see for miles and miles and it's just more trees, millions of them, and distant, lonely mountains. Up there, there's barely a trail, and Christian leads them by following cairns instead, little piles of rocks every thirty feet or so that lead the way across bare rock, up over craggy peaks and down into steep gulches. Sometimes, Christian misses the next cairn, and they all have spread out and search for the way forward, except it's usually just Lucas and sometimes Dawn who help Amber look; Warden and Evan and Brandon and Kyla hang back and make fun of the counselors and throw rocks off the mountain, and Brielle stays quiet and keeps to herself.

It's windy on the ridges, and cold, and the emptiness and the height and the barren, alien landscape kind of freak Dawn out, which is why she helps Lucas help the counselors look for the next cairn. It's like she hears a voice inside her head saying *You aren't supposed to be here*, and the sooner they can get back down into the rain forest, the better.

Dawn doesn't like the ridges. They give her a bad feeling. But the rain forest isn't much better, or the rough rivers they have to balance across on fallen tree trunks, the cliffs they have to scramble their way up and down, tottering for balance with their heavy packs, the marshy meadows with their sticky, stinky mud and their lingering mosquitoes and blackflies, the loose rocks and slippery bare roots on the trails that give out from under you, twisting your ankles, then uneven ground under your sleeping pad that hurts your neck when you're trying to sleep, the too-cold night and the too-hot daytime, the taste of the lake water even after you filter it, the dirt on your clothes and your smelly, unwashed body, your limp, stringy hair, the blisters on your feet and the bug bites on the rest of you, the way Christian makes fun of you and how Evan and Brandon whisper to each other when they look at you, the weird sounds in the forest at night, and the wondering what you'd do if Christian and Amber suddenly died or you got separated and had to survive by yourself and,

above all,

the loneliness.

16.

DAWN HAS A LOT OF TIME to think while she is enduring the Out of the Wild forced march regimen and the sensation of slowly starving to death.

Most of the time, she's pretty homesick. Not so much for Cam, of course, and she's still mad at Wendy, too, because any mom who'd kidnap her daughter and send her out into this bullshit doesn't deserve to be missed.

She misses Bryce, though, her little brother. And her nana, her grandmother on her dad's side, who lives in Chicago and who Dawn doesn't get to see very often but who she loves more than anyone else in the world, except maybe Bryce.

Dawn tortures herself, thinking about her nana.

She thinks about how she went to visit her nana in Chicago the summer before this one, how she always used to visit her as a kid and it was the most fun ever, how they'd walk along the lakeshore and go to the museums and eat pizza and just, you know, hang out.

And she thinks about how she didn't visit Nana this summer because she bailed on her parents and was crashing at Julian's and she kept meaning to find a way to get in touch with Nana and go visit without her mom finding out but there was always something else more important and she just never got around to it and now it's too late and she wasted her summer.

And then Dawn thinks about how her nana isn't sick or getting frail or anything crazy, but she *is* getting older, and Dawn won't see her until next summer at the earliest, probably, and what if Dawn gave up her last chance to spend time with her nana because she was too busy getting stoned and hooking up with Julian and sneaking into clubs and more or less causing mayhem?

And maybe it's the hiking and the fatigue or the trauma of the whole experience, or maybe it's just general loneliness, but that whole line of thinking makes Dawn VERY SAD.

Which is probably the whole point of all this hiking in the first place.

Dawn thinks about Bryce, too.

She thinks about how her little brother just started high school this month and how he's probably scared out of his mind and has nobody to talk to.

She thinks about how her whole family has known Bryce is gay pretty much from birth but how Bryce hasn't officially, you know, *come out* or anything, and she hopes the kids in high school aren't being assholes about that.

She thinks about how lonely and scared she was when she started high school and how it was only her dad who really helped her get over the loneliness and the fear and how Bryce doesn't have their dad to turn to, and he doesn't even have Dawn anymore, either.

She thinks about the last time she saw Bryce, when she made Julian drive her home so she could pick up a dress she wanted to wear to Post Malone that night, and Cam and Wendy were supposed to be not at home but they were at home anyway, but Dawn was pretty stoned and really wanted that dress, so she tried to sneak in and grab it without anyone noticing, and the whole plan backfired when Cam came out of the bathroom and saw her and said her name and then Wendy came rushing out into the living room to try to stop her from leaving, and a scuffle ensued and a loud altercation, and Wendy grabbed Dawn's arm and Dawn wrenched it away, and then Wendy grabbed the dress and Dawn screamed something mean at her and Wendy screamed something just as mean back, and there was Cam trying to step in between them, trying to break it up, Cam sticking his nose into family business where he wasn't welcome, as always. And then Dawn broke loose and just as she ran out the door she caught sight of Bryce in the corner, looking up from the book he'd been trying to read on the couch, and he was staring at Dawn with such, like, *sadness* and *distress* that it nearly stopped Dawn dead, shocked her so bad that she wanted to turn around and go running to him and wrap him up in a hug and apologize for being such a bitch and for messing up the family so much; she wanted to tell him she was coming back home and she was staying this time, and everything was going to be fine, was going to be wonderful again like it was when they were kids.

But she didn't, of course. She turned her back on her brother and ran out the front door and down the steps to where Julian was waiting in his Jeep, and Julian peeled off as Cam and Wendy watched from the doorway, and Dawn settled into the shotgun seat with the dress in her lap and she didn't look back.

And the worst part: somehow when Wendy and Dawn were fighting they'd torn the fabric, so Dawn didn't even get to wear the dress to the show that night. She'd thrown it in the back of Julian's closet instead and never looked at it again, and it's probably still there now, buried under trash and dirty laundry, waiting to never be worn again.

———

Dawn thinks about a lot while she's hiking. But she never thinks about her dad.

She just can't.

17.

AFTER SIX DAYS OF HIKING, a million bug bites, and too many blisters to mention, Dawn and the rest of the Out of the Wild Bear Pack follow Christian and Amber out of the rain forest and into a clearing. At the far end of the clearing are a couple of buildings and, beyond, a long gravel road.

Dawn recognizes these buildings. This is where Steve brought Dawn after she got off the plane, where Tanya strip-searched her and stole her phone and gave her the tarp. This is Out of the Wild HQ.

"Don't get any ideas," Christian says, watching the glint of recognition take hold on Dawn's face. "We're just here to re-supply, nothing else."

He's lying, a little bit. As the Pack comes out of the woods, Steve emerges from one of the buildings and waves to Christian and Amber and unlocks a big sliding door, and inside Dawn can see piles of food and supplies stacked up like in a warehouse.

And shirts. Lots of colored Bear Pack shirts.

"Kind of a slacker week for this pack," Christian says, picking up a red T-shirt from a pile and handing it to Evan. "Evan's the only promotion, guys. Better luck next week."

Evan snatches the red shirt from Christian's hands. He peels off his orange shirt and mimes wiping his ass with it, standing there shirtless and skeleton skinny, whooping at Brandon like he's just won the lottery.

"Suck it, Brando," he crows. "Black Bear, what?"

Brandon shoots Evan the finger. "Get dressed, faggot," he says. "Nobody wants to see that."

As Christian says, there are no other promotions. Dawn remains a Bear Cub. Brandon's still a Brown Bear, and he doesn't look thrilled about it. Lucas and Brielle are still Black Bears, but they don't seem to care.

The Polar Bears, though, are *pissed.*

Warden and Kyla stand in the back, whispering to each other and glaring at Christian and Amber. Dawn figures they probably have a good reason to be mad; she's not sure about Warden, but Kyla's been here for more than three months.

Christian only keeps me around because he likes looking at my ass, Kyla said. Dawn's starting to think that might be true.

After the promotions (or lack thereof), the group resupplies. Christian and Amber hand out food and clean clothes to everyone, and then each member of the Pack gets fifteen minutes in the little bathroom inside headquarters to wash and brush his/her teeth and otherwise freshen up.

This is so nobody looks completely ratchet in the ensuing

photographs, which Out of the Wild sends to every group member's family and/or parole officer to prove that their precious baby/repeat offender is still alive and didn't fall off a cliff yet.

Dawn scowls at the camera and Christian behind it and hopes when Cam and Wendy see the photo they feel so terribly guilty they bring her home early.

But Christian just chuckles. "Your folks read the brochure," he says. "They know this ain't summer camp."

Then he tosses her a headlamp.

"Congratulations on a decent first week," he says. "There's your reward."

Dawn stares at the headlamp. "*This* is my reward?" she says. "Where's my freaking *tent*?"

Christian lowers the camera. "Oh, right," he says. "Your *tent*."

"You said if I did okay, I wouldn't have to sleep under a tarp anymore," Dawn tells him. "That's what you said."

"You're right," Christian says, but his voice is that kind of sticky sweet that lets Dawn know he's bullshitting. "How stupid of me. What if I book you a suite at the Ritz to make up for it, Dawn? Would that be okay?"

Dawn stares at him. "You said," she says.

"You've been here for six days," Christian says, his voice hard again. "You've got to work a little harder if you want to earn that tent, Dawn."

Then he raises the camera again.

Looks back at the rest of the group.

"*Next!*"

The resupply and the rest of it takes maybe a couple of hours. It's nice to get clean clothes and to wash your face with hot water, but it doesn't last, and then Christian and Amber are telling the group to pack up again, and Dawn's struggling to fit all of the new food into her stupid makeshift tarp backpack, and Christian and Amber confer over a map briefly and then seem to come to a decision.

"Okay, Pack," Christian says, squaring his shoulders. "Say goodbye to civilization for another week."

There's nothing but grumbles and muttered swear words in response. But Christian doesn't hear it. He's already disappeared down a trail into the rain forest again.

18.

NOTHING MUCH HAPPENS over the next week. That's the beauty of the Out of the Wild program. You hike and sleep and hike and sleep and you're tired and sore and hungry all the time and every day just fades into the next.

The Pack hikes through the rain forest and they camp every night, and aside from a few more blisters and bug bites, nothing much changes.

Dawn hikes with Lucas, most of the time. They linger toward the back, but usually Kyla's behind them and sometimes Brandon and Evan. Amber usually brings up the rear, to make sure nobody gets lost or, you know, tries to escape.

Warden is always at the front of the Pack. He's tall and muscular and capable, and Brandon and Evan seem drawn to him. They're always in his orbit, and since Dawn's kind of weirded out by Brandon and Evan, she never goes near Warden.

Warden doesn't say much around the campfire.

He broods.

He knows what he's doing out here, though; that's for certain.

And he's pretty cute.

But Dawn doesn't think about Warden much. She's too busy enjoying hanging with Lucas.

Lucas is goofy. He has funny stories to tell Dawn about life back home in Fort Collins, and he likes country music and sings songs in a terrible cowboy yodel until Dawn's ears are nearly bleeding and she's begging him to stop, but she's laughing while she does it because he's so freaking *into* it—and she'd never tell him, but he's actually a pretty good singer, when he's being serious.

(And even when he's not being serious, his terrible singing takes her mind off her blisters and her aching muscles and her empty stomach, and it feels good to, you know, laugh every now and then.)

Among Lucas's talents is he does a pretty good imitation of Christian's ghoul voice. *"Bear Cub,"* he tells Dawn when she's slacking. *"Pick up the pace, you're falling behind."* It's exactly what Christian would say, and how Christian would say it, and Lucas even gets this look on his face like Christian, like he's got a stick so far up his ass it's propping his head up.

It doesn't make Dawn walk any faster, but it does make her laugh.

It's good to laugh out here.

It makes Dawn almost feel almost normal.

19.

AMBER FALLS IN STEP BESIDE DAWN and Lucas a few days into their second week on the trail. "Hey, Lucas," she says. "Do you mind if I talk to Dawn on her own for a little bit?"

Lucas is in the middle of telling some story in Christian's voice.

"Sure, no problem," he says, and it comes out in Christian's voice and he immediately goes red and looks panicked. "I mean, shit. Sorry."

Amber laughs. "No worries," she says. "That's Christian, right? It's pretty good."

Lucas looks down at the ground. "Please don't demote me."

"I'm not going to bust you," Amber says, rolling her eyes. "Come on, dude. Just don't let Christian hear you, or you'll be a Bear Cub for life."

Lucas exhales and looks relieved.

"Now, can I get some time alone with Dawn, please?" Amber asks him.

Lucas nods. "Yeah, of course," he says. "I'm *really* sorry."

Then he hurries up the trail a little bit. Joins Kyla where she's hiking. Dawn watches him start a conversation with Kyla and feels stupidly jealous.

But Amber's touching her shoulder.

"So, Dawn," she says. "How are you doing?"

It's a stupid question. The answer is self-evident.

How am I doing? I'm marooned in the woods doing forced marches until I die, Amber. I hate everything.

How are you doing?

But Dawn knows that Amber isn't going to be satisfied with *I hate everything* as an answer. So she shrugs. "My feet hurt," she says. "And I'm *really* hungry."

Amber looks at her. "Uh-huh." It's like she's waiting for an answer that isn't just complaining. Dawn gives it a beat, but Amber's kind of stubborn.

Finally, Dawn sighs. "I'm fine, I guess," she says. "I want to go home, but I doubt you're going to let me do that, so, whatever."

"Come on," Amber says. "You don't want to go home now, do you? Isn't this kind of fun?"

This time, Dawn stares at Amber until Amber kind of laughs and shakes her head. "Well, you're right, we can't let you go yet," she says. "Not until you're a Grizzly. But we'll get you there. I promise."

"Okay," Dawn says. "I mean, whatever. Is this what you wanted to talk to me about?"

There's another part of the Out of the Wild MO that I haven't brought up yet. It's the part where they try to get you to TALK about your FEELINGS.

It's the part where you EXPLORE why you're so ANGRY and why it makes you ACT OUT.

Sometimes this happens in a GROUP SETTING and sometimes it's ONE-ON-ONE.

Right now, for Dawn and Amber, it's ONE-ON-ONE.

***

"Your file says you ran away from home," Amber tells Dawn as they hike up the side of a narrow, rocky river. "Do you want to talk about that?"

"Not really," Dawn says. She's hoping she can just stonewall Amber, deflect until it's time to stop for lunch or dinner or make camp or resupply or go home.

She is aware this is probably going to be impossible.

"I also read that you've got a bit of a drug habit," Amber says. "Do you want to tell me about that?"

"No thank you," Dawn says.

"I guess there was a guy, too," Amber says. "Somebody older? Your parents were worried he was a bad influence."

"You mean my mom," Dawn says before she can stop herself. "I don't have parents. My dad's dead."

This is THE WRONG THING TO SAY to a person like Amber. Dawn knows it as soon as she says it. She can see how Amber immediately perks up. "I heard that, too," Amber says. "I'm so sorry. It's been a couple of years, right?"

Dawn feels the first tingle of panic. "I don't want to talk about it," she says.

"I get that," Amber tells her. "I really do. But it might help, you know, talking to someone? You can't just keep these feelings bottled up inside."

Sure I can, Dawn thinks. *Just try me.*

"I know it must have been hard on you," Amber says. "According to your file, you started acting out shortly after your dad passed."

Dawn feels it like sandpaper on her nerves. Rubbing grit into her, making her squirm. "I don't want to talk about it," she says again. Tries to shut down, go flat and numb and lifeless.

"I know you're not a bad kid, Dawn," Amber says. "Your mom says in your file that you're smart and creative and kind, and hey, I can sense that just spending time around you. I'd love to help you get back to that person we both know you are, if you'd let me."

Dawn thinks that Amber doesn't know anything about her, that she's full of shit, that she's not qualified to say anything about how Dawn should lead her life just because she read a freaking file.

But she also wants to believe Amber. She wants to believe there's a way out of this that doesn't involve screaming fits with your mom and sex with drug dealers. She wants to believe life is going to get better.

What she *doesn't* want to do is have to talk about her dad. Not now or ever. Not to Amber or anyone else. She doesn't want to think about him, period.

She just can't.

"I don't want to talk about it," she tells Amber again. And this time Amber seems to actually hear her.

"That's okay," the counselor says. She smiles at Dawn brightly and touches her shoulder. "Another time, maybe," she says.

I doubt it, Dawn thinks, but she doesn't say anything. She just quickens her pace and tries to catch up with Lucas and Kyla.

And leaves Amber in her dust.

20.

A WEEK PASSES. Dawn spends it mostly with Lucas. She avoids Amber and *really* avoids Christian. She figures out, mostly, how to set up her tarp. She eats more rice and lentils than she ever thought possible, and still it doesn't feel like enough.

She goes to bed hungry.

Her pants start to feel noticeably looser.

A week passes.

At the end of the week, the Out of the Wild Bear Pack staggers back into headquarters, and there's a new recruit waiting for them, spiffed out in bright-yellow "Bear Club" gear. He's standing outside the headquarters buildings with the guy who brought Dawn from the airport, Steve. He watches the group stagger in from the woods and his eyes just get wider and wider.

"Hey, group," Steve says when the Pack reaches the buildings. "Meet Alex."

Alex is from Spokane. He's tall and looks fit and Dawn thinks he should be okay in the woods. But he's looking at the Pack like they're a horde of zombies. Or, like, prisoners in some wartime camp.

Alex doesn't look scared. He doesn't look like the kind of guy who gets scared.

But the way he's looking at Dawn and the others, Dawn can tell he's at least, you know, *unnerved*.

Alex shares his Origin Story as they stand around outside headquarters.

"I'm from Spokane, like that dude said," he tells the Pack while they wait for Christian to take their pictures and give them new gear. "Inner city, as much as you could say that there is one there."

He says it was stealing that got him dragged out here. "Stickup kids," he says, kind of grinning. "Me and this guy I was kind of sort of seeing. We'd steal anything that wasn't nailed down."

He shrugs. "Wasn't anything violent," he says. "We were just bored. Kind of for the challenge of it, nothing else. Steal a bunch of shit and go somewhere and hook up."

He meets Dawn's eyes.

"Anyway, we got caught, and my man blamed me for everything. And then the youth counselor asked me did I like camping."

Alex says, "I told her I didn't care for it."

He smiles again.

"Wrong answer."

The rest of the Pack kind of laughs with Alex. As far as Origin Stories go, it's not the worst thing they've ever heard.

And Alex doesn't seem altogether miserable to be out here. And he kind of looks like he knows what he's doing. He seems to know how to bundle all of his stuff in his tarp, anyway.

Alex seems like a Good Dude.

He's not bitter, at least.

(Dawn wonders how long that will last.)

21.

BRANDON GETS HIS PROMOTION to Black Bear this week, probably just so Evan will stop teasing him. The clouds above Warden and Kyla get darker. Even Lucas looks disappointed.

But Amber takes Dawn aside. "We can't promote you yet," she tells Dawn. "But you did have a pretty good week. So me and Christian decided you were due for a reward."

Dawn wonders just how much input Christian had in this decision. Somehow, she doesn't think he cares. But Amber clearly does. She actually looks *happy* for Dawn, like this is some big event in her life.

Amber touches Dawn on the shoulder. "Come on," she says, grinning. "Rewards are in the cabin." She gestures through the open cabin door. After a beat, Dawn sighs and follows her inside.

—————

The rewards are pretty basic. Dawn's options are:

a)   a hiking backpack, or
b)   a tent

"You also get some better food," Amber tells her. "So you don't have to eat lentils all the time. And whatever you don't pick this time, you can take next week when we come back to resupply. Just keep doing great, like you're already doing, and you'll be kitted out in no time."

The tent and the backpack are laid out like game show prizes on the floor of the little supply room. Dawn looks from one to the other and back again.

(Wonders again how she arrived at this stupid place in her life.)

Amber nudges her. "So, what do you think?" she asks. "Which reward do you choose?"

Dawn looks at the tent and the backpack and wishes she could trade either one for a plane ticket to Chicago. But that clearly isn't happening.

She looks outside, where the rest of the Pack is sitting on the grass in the clearing, or leaned up against *their* backpacks, taking advantage of the break to rest a little bit. They all have backpacks *and* tents.

Dawn catches Lucas's eye, and he gives her a little wave and jogs over. "What's up?" he asks.

"Dawn's trying to decide which reward to choose," Amber tells him, fully buying into the game show host role. "Do you have any advice for her, Lucas?"

Lucas (dork) takes the question very seriously. "I mean, it sucks lugging your stuff around in a tarp," he says, scratching his head. "But my life really got better when I upgraded to my tent. *So* many less bug bites."

"So I should take the tent," Dawn says. "That's what you're saying?"

Lucas screws up his face. Turns around and looks up at the sky like the clouds have answers.

"I mean, it's probably not going to rain too much this week, right?" he says, looking at Amber for confirmation. "And the bugs really aren't so bad now that summer's over."

So I should take the pack? Dawn wants to ask him. *Come on, man, help me out here.* She doesn't get the chance, though, because Christian walks into the supply room from the office, eating a microwaved burrito and scratching his chest.

"We ready to move out?" he asks Amber.

"Just about," Amber replies. "Just waiting on Dawn to choose her reward."

Christian chews his burrito. It smells absolutely delicious, and for a split second, Dawn contemplates murdering him for half of it. But he's bigger than her, and she doesn't have any weapons.

Christian keeps scratching. "We gotta move out," he tells Amber. "If she doesn't want the reward, she doesn't have to have either; I don't care."

Amber gives Dawn a look that's half apology, half exasperation—though with Christian or Dawn, Dawn isn't sure. "We're getting there, Christian," she says. "You round up the others and we'll finish up in here."

Christian finishes his burrito. "Don't keep us waiting," he says. "Lots of ground to cover."

He ambles away, and Amber's eyes meet Dawn's again, and

now Dawn's reasonably certain it's Christian who Amber's tired of, not her.

"So what do you think?" Amber says again, her voice a little less cheery. "The pack or the tent?"

<hr/>

Dawn chooses the pack. She's sick of having to tie everything up in that stupid tarp, and anyway, it probably won't rain, and even if it does, she has Lucas's tent pegs to keep the tarp down.

That's what she tells herself, anyway.

As Amber mentioned, part of Dawn's reward is she gets some actual food this week, too, instead of just a sack of rice and whatever. Amber gives her six little boxes that look like Army surplus, and smiles another game show host smile that would be super irritating if Dawn wasn't so sick of freaking rice.

Anyway, Dawn stuffs everything in her new backpack, and then she joins the rest of the Pack on the grass behind the buildings for pictures, and then it's time to go again and Christian's leading them to this week's trail.

"You're going to love this one," he tells the group, grinning that ghoulish smile. "I promise, this week is going to be *fun*."

22.

THE NEW TRAIL CHRISTIAN CHOOSES seems to go straight *up* through the rain forest, over like a million switchbacks on a steep, narrow path. Dawn's new pack helps, but the straps dig into her skin through her yellow T-shirt as she climbs and she's tired and she's hungry and she thinks about Christian's burrito and decides she would trade her new pack and her clean yellow shirts just for a bite of it.

But there are no burritos in Dawn's future. There's only hiking.

The new guy, Alex, turns out to be a pretty good hiker, just as Dawn suspected. She can see his yellow shirt keeping pace with Christian and Warden at the head of the Pack, even with no backpack and just a stupid tarp to carry his stuff.

Dawn kind of hates him already.

The Pack makes camp for the night on the shore of a little lake just below the tree line, beside a large boulder field that looks something like Mordor, rocks the size of dump trucks scattered around the mountain slope. A hundred feet up the slope, the trees end, and it's just bare rock and grassy moss and a towering cliff face, high above. Beside it, a rocky spine of a ridgeline leads off behind the trees. The clouds are pouring over it as the last light of day disappears. It looks naked and barren and soulless; Dawn shivers and hopes they don't have to go up there.

"Fart Mountain." Lucas's voice scares her out of her trance. Dawn stifles a shriek and spins around to shove him.

"Don't do that," she says, angry at first but not really, especially after Lucas gives her that big white smile. "Wait, what?" she says. "Did you say Fart Mountain?"

Lucas nods solemnly. "Yes, ma'am. Spell it like it sounds."

Dawn points up the boulder field. "You mean that cliff up there?"

"No," Lucas replies. "You can't see Fart Mountain, yet. It's still hidden behind the trees. But tomorrow, if it's not too cloudy when we get up into the alpine, then you'll see it." He grins at her again. "And it will scare the ever-loving shit out of you."

This actually makes Dawn kind of nervous, but she pretends like she doesn't care.

"What the fuck is Fart Mountain, and why should I be scared?" she says. "And that's not its actual name is it?"

"It might be; you don't know," Lucas says. "No one ever said what its real name is, so who's to say it wasn't named after a fart?"

"You sound like Evan and Brandon," Dawn replies. "All this fart talk, what are you, twelve?"

Lucas's smile disappears. "I'm just saying, it's a scary freaking mountain," he tells her. "I call it Fart Mountain to, like, ease the tension or whatever, because up close and personal? It's terrifying. You'll see."

Dawn looks out through the trees again, even though it's getting dark and there's no hope of seeing the mountain, whatever it's called, anyway. "How do you know that's where we're going?" she asks Lucas.

"This trail only goes in one direction," he tells her. "Ask Kyla or Warden; they've done it before. Ask anyone; why do you think Christian's so excited? He knows it's going to be torture. It's three days to get to the top of Fart Mountain, three days to get out of the bush again. The toughest hike in this part of the state, and we haven't even barely started yet."

Lucas doesn't look like a big happy dog anymore. He looks pretty scared actually.

"Have you done it before?" Dawn asks him. "Climbed, you know, the mountain?"

(She's not calling it "Fart Mountain.")

Lucas shakes his head. "Not yet."

"So how do you know it's so rough? I call bullshit."

"Ask Kyla," he says. "She did it, the first month she was here. She said the summit's so high, there's snow up there all summer long. Half of the Pack nearly froze to death."

Dawn doesn't say anything. She doesn't look at Lucas.

"I mean, hey, she's probably lying," Lucas says after a beat. "Either way, I guess we're going to find out."

He wanders off, after that, though Dawn barely notices. She's watching the night fall above the dark treetops, feeling the sudden chill in the air.

And that's when she hears the bear.

23.

DAWN'S IN A LITTLE CLEARING away from the campsite, gathering firewood, and at first, she thinks it's just one of the other group members making all that noise through the trees. One of the boys, probably, or maybe even Christian. Somebody big, anyway.

She watches the tops of the trees sway and listens to the leaves rustle, and maybe it's residual fear from Lucas's Fart Mountain proclamation, or maybe it's instinct, but something twinges in her stomach as she begins to realize it's probably impossible for a teenager—or even an adult—to break so many tree branches so easily.

"Hello?" she calls into the bushes, and there is no answer, and suddenly the rest of the group seems to have disappeared, leaving her alone with whatever's coming—slowly, steadily, *heavily*—toward her.

And then the trees part, and the bear wanders out into Dawn's little patch of space.

It's a black bear. Amber says there are no grizzlies in Out of the Wild territory, which is good, because Christian swears that grizzly bears will happily kill and eat you.

(Black bears, Amber says, just want to be left alone.)

This black bear hasn't seen Dawn yet. It's just nosing through the bushes, snorting and snuffling, and even though it's enormous and could probably kill Dawn with one swipe of its paw, it doesn't really look mean or even seem to care that Dawn's there, and for a moment she starts to believe that maybe it'll just wander right past her, without even seeing her. Without even trying to eat her.

But then Dawn shifts her weight, and a twig snaps beneath her boot. And the bear stops, suddenly, and looks across the clearing at her.

And Dawn hears the low growl begin in its throat.

24.

ONE OF THE BOOKS Dawn's been lugging around since she got here is called *Don't Get Eaten*. It's the only one she's actually bothered to read, mostly because it's small, and also because she really doesn't want to get, you know, *eaten*, by bears or cougars or wolves or anything else that lurks in this ungodly place.

And Amber's always preaching bear safety, so Dawn knows a little bit about how to deal with an unexpected bear.

She knows, for instance, she's supposed to stay calm. She knows she's supposed to speak to the bear and identify herself and let the bear know she's not food.

"Hello, Mr. Bear," Dawn says, hoping the bear doesn't hear how her voice is shaking. "I'm just a friendly girl over here, not your dinner."

According to the book, this should convince the bear that he's better off moving on. But if the bear sticks around, Dawn remembers, she's supposed to make herself big and back away slowly.

The bear does not seem to be moved by her introduction.

"Just asking you not to eat me, Mr. Bear," Dawn tells it. She waves her hands above her head and takes a step backward, keeping her voice calm and her movements slow.

The bear growls again. Louder this time. It stands up on its hind legs and peers across the clearing at her and yawns, and Dawn can see drool in its mouth, and sharp, yellow teeth.

"Don't eat me, Mr. Bear," Dawn says again. *"Please?"*

But the bear doesn't seem to be listening. It drops down to all four legs again, and begins to approach her, and even though it's just walking, it's faster than Dawn expected, and closer, too. It's thirty feet away and closing fast, faster than she can walk backward.

(*Don't run*, the book says. *Don't scream or make sudden movements.*)

Dawn's not sure she can control herself; she's too scared. She's half afraid she's going to pee her pants.

She's. From. *Suburban. Sacramento.*

The bear keeps coming. It's looking right at her, and now she can smell its terrible breath and see right into its eyes, and it looks mean and angry with her, like a friendly discussion isn't going to scare it away.

Dawn's still backing up, trying to remember what she's supposed to do next, when she backs into a log and loses her balance.

And as she falls flat on her ass, she glances to her left and sees *another* bear emerge from the trees, a smaller bear.

A baby bear.

And that's when she knows she's screwed.

Dawn screams.

25.

A MOTHER BEAR IS DANGEROUS, the book in Dawn's pack says. *Especially if she perceives you as a threat to her cubs.*

Dawn wants to explain to this approaching mama bear that she's in no way a threat to anybody. That she's actually *literally* a Bear Cub herself. That she just wants to get back to her group, and then down off this mountain, and then back on a plane to Sacramento.

But she's flat on her ass and the mama bear's approaching. The time for conversation is over.

If a black bear attacks you, the book says, *fight back.*

Fight for your life.

Dawn reaches around for a weapon. A stick or a rock or anything she can find. The bear keeps coming toward her, snuffling and snarling, and Dawn screams and she can hear voices behind her, somewhere in the forest, but they seem so far away, and the bear is much closer, and she can't find anything she can use to defend herself.

She scrabbles backward, over the log that tripped her. Finds a broken tree branch and lifts it and swings wildly at the bear, and the branch is rotted through and splits in half as she swings it, and she's crying now and screaming her throat raw.

"Help!" she says. "Damn it, somebody help me!"

The bear looms above her. From this angle, it's huge; it's all Dawn can see. Its harsh breathing is all Dawn can hear. And it suddenly seems stupid that this is how she's going to die, eaten by a bear—a *black* bear—in the middle of nowhere, screaming for her life and probably peeing her pants.

And then a gunshot cracks behind her.

It's *loud*.

The bear goes stiff, and seems to forget about Dawn. Looks past her into the trees as another shot fires. As Amber races into the clearing and drags Dawn to her feet. As Christian and Lucas and maybe some other people burst in beside her, yelling loudly at the bear and waving their arms.

A third shot goes off, and Dawn momentarily goes deaf.

The bear looks around. Looks back at its cub, which is now racing away, terrified, out of the other side of the clearing. The bear opens its mouth and makes some kind of noise that Dawn can't really hear because her ears are still ringing from the shots.

Then it turns and lopes off across the clearing, following its cub.

It stops once, and looks back, and its eyes fall on Dawn again. And it stares at Dawn for a long moment, like it's staring right into her soul.

And then it turns around and disappears into the trees.

26.

"I DON'T UNDERSTAND," Dawn says, when Amber and Lucas have helped her back to the campfire, and after she's unsuccessfully petitioned the counselors to abandon the hike, bring the group out of bear country and back to civilization.

"If Christian shot the bear, why wasn't it injured?"

Christian laughs. He looks utterly unfazed by the whole experience. "I didn't shoot the bear," he tells her. "You think they'd let you kids anywhere near a *gun?*"

Dawn stares at him. "No, what the hell," she says. "I heard the shots."

Christian and Amber swap looks. And then Christian reaches into his pocket. He pulls out something the size and shape of a pen. "Bear banger," Amber explains. "It sounds like a gun. Most of the time it's enough to scare a bear away."

Christian grins at her. "*Most* of the time," he says.

"And if that doesn't work, there's bear spray," Lucas adds quickly. "Right? You guys are at least carrying bear spray, aren't you?"

"Sure," Christian says, and he seems to meet Dawn's eyes the same way as the bear did. "And most of the time that works pretty well, too."

Dawn shivers, and stares into the campfire. She's already pretty sure she's never sleeping again.

27.

THE BEAR DOESN'T COME BACK. But Dawn doesn't sleep much that night anyway.

It still sucks sleeping under that tarp, her new pack notwithstanding, and it's starting to get really cold when the sun goes down. She spends most of the night curled up in her sleeping bag, freezing, listening to the sound of the trees moving in the wind, and branches snapping, and worrying the bear will come back.

And when she's sick of worrying about bears, she starts to worry about Fart Mountain.

Of course, she doesn't know much about Fart Mountain other than it has the world's stupidest name, so she actually moves on pretty quickly to her *other* big concerns, like whether she'll ever get to see her nana again, and whether Bryce is getting bullied at school without her. She spends the time feeling helpless and powerless and lonely and hungry and sad.

(And cold. Really cold.)

And in between all the worrying, she spends some time, being mad, too, at Christian and Amber and all the other Out of the Wild d-bags. At the bear for trying to eat her, and at Lucas for putting the fear of Fart Mountain in her. At Wendy for marrying Cam, and Cam and Wendy both for kidnapping her and sending her to this awful frigid place. And when she gets done being mad at everyone she can think of, Dawn turns her anger on the person who deserves it most.

(And that person is Dawn herself.)

Dawn's dad would be alive, if it wasn't for Dawn.

That's just a plain fact.

Everything bad that's happened to Dawn afterward?

She deserves it.

28.

THERE IS NO COFFEE in Out of the Wild.

I don't think I mentioned that part.

Sure, Christian gets to drink his coffee in the morning, but nobody else does. Not even Amber, though Dawn's pretty sure that's a choice.

There's, like, herbal tea, but it's weak as shit and not even close to adequate for the situations described herein. Right now, and most mornings, Dawn needs like a quad espresso and maybe a shot of Jack.

But there's no whiskey in Out of the Wild either.

(Duh.)

Anyway, Dawn staggers out from her tarp the next morning, foggy-headed and somehow, miraculously, not eaten by any bears, and she joins the rest of the Pack with the morning chores—

(get dressed, brush teeth, pee in the woods somewhere, pump water for your water bottle, build the fire, cook breakfast, etc., etc.)

—and then she packs up her tarp in her brand-new back-pack—

(which is already starting to get smeared with a little bit of mud, just like her brand-new yellow shirt)

—and they kick the fire out and fall in behind Christian, and Christian leads them from the campsite and into the trees again, through the middle of bear territory on a narrow game trail that winds around the shore of the little lake and up the side of the boulder field toward the edge of the forest and the ridgeline beyond.

And by eight in the morning, Dawn and the rest of the Bear Pack are up on the ridge. And Dawn hopes that means the real bears, at least, are behind them.

It's kind of overcast this morning, so Dawn can't see Fart Mountain right away.

What she can see is a long, arching ridgeline of barren, empty rock, punctuated by a few lumpy, pimply hills and a couple of deep chasms. On either side, the ridge drops away sharply into empty forest and wide, lonely valleys. Aside from the cairns that mark the path every so often, there is no sign of human life.

(You're not supposed to be here.)

The Pack takes a few minutes for water at the start of the ridge. Dawn spends it peering in vain through the cloud cover for any sign of Fart Mountain. Then Christian tells them to mount up again, and they're off, following the top of the ridge from cairn to cairn, a long line of misfit teens yawning and stumbling toward an uncertain destination.

———————

Dawn's *really* tired. She's got enough on her plate trying to put one foot in front of the other and not, like, fall off a cliff or twist her ankle on a rock. She's following Evan, who's right in front of her, and that's pretty well sapping her mental capacity at the moment. So she doesn't really notice much of anything else.

(Though later on, she's *really* going to wish she did.)

She doesn't notice, for instance, how the ridge they're hiking on joins another ridge after a couple of hours. She doesn't notice how there's really only one good way to traverse this particular chasm she's struggling down, and how the route isn't exactly obvious from the bottom. She doesn't notice how Lucas has sped up a little bit, and is talking with Alex, leaving her a ways behind, and she *definitely* doesn't notice how Warden's kind of lagging behind everyone, dawdling at the back of the Pack when he's usually at the front.

Dawn's just focused on staying upright, for now. And in a few days, she's going to hate herself for it.

In the meantime, though, she's about to nearly die.

29.

IT HAPPENS BECAUSE SHE'S TIRED. She's tired and the ground is slippery and her legs are sore and her new pack isn't sitting right on her back and she's trying to fake her way down this rocky ravine that kind of cuts the ridge in half.

Honestly, it would be terrifying even if you *weren't* half-dead from exhaustion and fear and didn't have crazy blisters on your feet. Dawn's standing on top of this ledge, staring straight down at a little half-assed trail that kind of clings to the rock face, barely wide enough for both of her size 6 hiking boots, much less that big freaking pack. One side is solid rock. The other is a sheer drop, fifty feet if she's lucky, punctuated by jagged shards of rock and stubby little trees that would probably impale you. Even Christian and Amber are taking it slow; Amber keeps looking back up the rocks at Dawn with a concerned look on her face, and shouting something about making sure to keep a good handhold and taking it slow and everything will be fine.

Easy for you to say, Dawn thinks. *You do this shit for a living.*

Anyway, Dawn's clinging to the ledge and reaching for her

next handhold and trying not to look down and trying not to think about falling—which only makes it worse, of course—and she's doing okay until she gets to this little section where the trail literally *ends* and there's just a gap in the rocks at her feet with a couple of handholds and then nothing but air and the long drop, and to get down to the next part of the trail she realizes she's going to have to let go of the rocks and turn around to face backward and, like, step *back* off the ledge and reach down blindly with her feet until she finds somewhere to step.

And the trail's only like six feet below her but then it's just another ledge with another long drop below that, so if she loses her grip or slips or whatever she'll probably bounce off the trail and keep falling until she lands, *splat*, at the bottom of the ravine.

Dawn's kind of hyperventilating. She stops at the gap and holds on to the rocks and wishes she were anywhere but here.

(Jail, for example.)

(Or even high school.)

She wishes she could turn around and run back up to the top of the ridge and follow the cairns back across the ridge and down the other side to the Out of the Wild home base, where there's a phone and vans and a road that leads somewhere where decisions like these won't ever be a part of her life.

And she might be trying it, too, if Warden and Brielle weren't stacked up on the trail behind/above her, grabbing hold of their own rocks for balance and waiting and watching her have a near nervous breakdown on the middle of this wall.

They're all laughing at you, she thinks. *They're standing there judging you, talking shit about you.*

They all think you're a big fucking loser.

Dawn can feel Warden's and Brielle's eyes on her. They don't say anything, but she can *feel* how they're staring. She closes her eyes—*fuck it*—and before she can think twice, she kind of awkwardly shuffles around so she's facing the rocks and her back's to the clouds, and then she takes a step back into open air and lets go of the cliff face with one hand and starts to lower herself down, feeling around with her toes for someplace to land.

And it's just as Dawn finds solid ground with her left foot and just as she lets go of the cliff with her other hand and starts to climb down that disaster strikes.

The ground gives way.

Dawn's foot slips.

Something in her backpack shifts and it fucks up her balance and sends her teetering backward, her arms windmilling the air, her hands grabbing at the rocks for anything to save her,

but

she's slipping too fast

falling out of control

she feels herself tripping backward

and

she knows this is it.

AUTHOR'S NOTE

WE HAVEN'T TALKED MUCH about Warden.

I mean, you know who he is and that he's a Polar Bear. You know that he's athletic and muscular and cute.

You might have guessed he'll play a bigger role in this story, eventually.

(It was probably the brooding that gave it away.)

But we haven't really seen much of Warden, not yet.

Not until now.

30.

SOMEONE GRABS DAWN'S HAND.

Arrests her fall.

Holds on to her, tight, just as she's bracing for impact. Just as she's mentally saying her goodbyes.

(*Bye, Nana. Bye, Bryce.*)

(*Fuck you, Cam.*)

Someone saves her life, holds her steady, stops her from falling and keeps her in place until her feet find firmer ground.

And Dawn kind of hangs there, hugging the rocks, breathing hard, wondering why she isn't dead, and she realizes she's still holding on to whoever just saved her.

And she looks up, and it's Warden. And Warden's staring down at her.

And Warden has the greenest eyes she's ever seen.

(Because of course he does.)

31.

"HOLD UP A SECOND."

Dawn's made it down to the bottom of the ravine and half-way up the other side. The rest of the Bear Pack is already at the top, chilling up on the ridge again, and Dawn is kind of in shock, half replaying that sick weightless feeling when she started to fall, and half replaying Warden's green eyes, that deep, serious stare.

He hadn't said anything, just held on to her until he was sure she was safe, and then he'd watched, his brow furrowed, as she lowered herself down the cliff and she'd touched down on the trail again and could feel herself blushing, her heart pounding rapid-fire like she'd just done a line, and she'd avoided his eyes and made her way down the rest of the ravine without looking back.

And frankly, Dawn's hoping she can just climb up the other side with the rest of the Pack and forget about what just transpired right there, forget how scared she is of these stupid heights and how embarrassed she is at messing up and nearly dying, forget the stupid butterflies in her stupid stomach that went haywire as soon as she realized it was Warden holding on to her, as soon as she realized she was literally safe in his arms.

But Warden has other ideas.

"Yo, hold up," he says again, and Dawn looks down the winding switchback trail to where Warden is steadily catching up to her, not breaking a sweat or even breathing heavily as he climbs.

(Dawn can see the muscles in his arms work as he pulls himself up, and how lean and solid his body looks under his shirt, and she feels herself blushing again and tries not to pay attention.)

(She looks away and continues up the trail.)

"Thanks," she calls over her shoulder, trying not to sound like she's just noticing that he's, you know, *hot*. "I almost bit it back there."

"Yeah," Warden says, and even his voice is sexy, deeper than it has any right to be, and as solemn and serious as the rest of him. "Hey, wait up a second."

"I'm good," Dawn replies. She doesn't slow down. "It's all good."

"No," Warden says. "It's not."

Dawn slows and looks back at him, kind of surprised. "It's not?"

"No." Warden closes the last ten feet or so. They're nearly at the top of the ridge; Dawn can see a cairn just above them where the wall levels out onto mostly flat rock again. She waits as Warden climbs up to her.

"Come here," he says, and gestures to the cairn. He squeezes past Dawn, and with nothing else to do, Dawn follows.

Warden is waiting at the top of the ravine, hands on his hips. He beckons Dawn to come closer. Dawn puts on a nonchalant face and does what Warden wants.

"Hey," she says.

Warden's still brooding. "You almost died back there," he tells her.

"Yeah, I know," Dawn says. "Thank you so much. If you hadn't caught me, I would be—"

"You know why?" Warden says.

"I—what?"

"Do you know why you fell?"

Dawn kind of shrugs. "I just, like, slipped a little bit. That trail was so narrow. Thank God you were there, huh?"

"No." Warden reaches out and Dawn flinches, like he's going to hit her or something. But he's only grabbing hold of her pack's shoulder straps.

"Your pack isn't tight enough," he says, and he grips the straps tight and tugs, hard enough that Dawn stumbles and nearly falls into him. The straps tighten around her, though, and she can feel the pack sitting closer to her body, firm and steady.

"Your weight shifted at the exact wrong possible moment and it ruined your balance," Warden says. "You have to make sure everything's done up right."

"Oh," Dawn replies, hating how small and childish her voice sounds.

Warden finishes with her shoulder straps. Reaches around

Dawn's side to her hips and pulls the straps there tight, too. There's nothing romantic about what he's doing, and yet it's possibly kind of sexy, how strong he is, and how serious, how he's obviously concerned about her.

(Or maybe it's just been too long since Dawn hooked up with anyone. Either way, she's immediately conscious of how close Warden's standing—and how bad she must smell.)

When Warden's done with the straps, he stands straight and examines her. "How does that feel?"

Dawn tests the straps. The backpack is sitting firm now, like it's an extension of her body. And Warden's green eyes are fixed on hers.

"Uh, good?" she says.

"'Uh, good?'" Suddenly there's a smirk in those green eyes. "Does it really feel okay, or are you just trying to get me away from you?" Warden cocks his head. "I might not be there to catch you, next time."

"No, it feels good," Dawn says. She twists and turns a little bit, and the pack moves with her, nothing shifting. "It feels solid. I think I'm good now. I think—"

She's about to say something else, but then she glances past Warden along the length of the ridge and beyond, where the clouds have suddenly parted in the distance revealing—

"Fart Mountain!" Dawn says before she can stop herself. (#FacePalm)

Warden blinks. "Fart . . . *Mountain?*" he says slowly.

Dawn looks back at the ravine they just climbed, wondering if it's too late to hurl herself from the top. She can feel herself blushing again, really bad. "Yeah, it's . . ." Dawn can't even. She just points. "That's what that mountain's called, right?"

Warden turns to see where she's pointing. It's the tallest peak in sight, just jagged rock reaching high into the clouds, mottled with little patches of snow here and there. There does not seem to be any easy way up, at least not anything visible at this distance, and just looking at it makes Dawn's stomach feel queasy.

Lucas was right. It's a scary freaking mountain.

But if Warden's afraid, he doesn't show it. "You mean the Raven's Claw?" he asks her. "You call that *Fart Mountain?*"

"*I* don't," Dawn hastens to assure him. "It's—that's what Lucas called it."

"Oh. *Lucas.*" Warden's lip curls into something like a smirk. "Yeah, I guess that checks out."

They look across the ridge toward where Lucas is hiking with Alex about a hundred feet away. As if he can hear them, Lucas stops and turns around, stares back at them, shading his eyes. He sees Dawn and then he sees Warden, and he doesn't look happy about it.

The two guys kind of stare at each other for a beat, and it's awkward AF.

"Why do you call it Raven's Claw?" Dawn asks Warden, to break the silence.

Warden blinks. "Because that's what it's called," he says, forgetting about Lucas. "I stole the counselors' map once. That's what it was labeled."

That answer makes enough sense that Dawn momentarily

misses the obvious follow-up question. "Wait, you *stole* the map?" she asks after a beat. "Do you still have it?"

Warden shakes his head. "Photographic memory, though."

"So you know where we are?"

"I know where we are, and I know where we're going," Warden tells her. Then he smirks again. "And I know how to get us out of here, too."

32.

DAWN HAS SO MANY QUESTIONS:

1. "How did you steal the map?"
2. "Are you seriously planning to escape?"
3. "Why don't you just wait and graduate?"
4. "What if you die?"

But mostly:

5. "Will you take me with you?"

She doesn't get a chance to ask any questions, though, because it's about at this point that Christian comes back up the trail to see what's taking them so long.

"What's taking you so long?" he demands. "You're holding everyone up."

Warden is unfazed. "Just fixing her straps, dude," he says. "Don't have a conniption."

Christian looks like he wants to argue the point, or at least the tone of the point. He doesn't, though. "Get a move on," he grumbles, and turns to lurch back along the ridge. "We don't want to be up here at nightfall, I promise you that."

Dawn watches the counselor retreat. *Even Christian is intimidated by Warden,* she realizes. *If anyone can escape this place, maybe it's him?*

Warden meets Dawn's eyes, gestures down the trail after Christian, one eyebrow raised like it's all a big joke. "Shall we?" he asks.

"We shall," Dawn replies. She turns to follow Christian, and starts back to join the rest of the Pack.

33.

"IT'S NOT CALLED FART MOUNTAIN," Dawn tells Lucas. "It's actually the Raven's Claw."

It's nearly nightfall. They've hiked across the ridge for most of the day, the mountain looming ominously in front of them the whole time. Near the end of the day, they took a side trail down a steep valley, descending back below the tree line and following a rocky little creek to the shore of another lake.

It's warmer down here, among the trees, the ridge staring down, impassive, from high above. There's enough wind that the bugs aren't so bad, and even the sight of the mountain reflected on the water is kind of pretty and peaceful, as long as you don't think about having to climb it.

The Pack sets up for the night on the lakeshore. Dawn follows Lucas into the woods to find firewood. It's the first time they've talked all day.

"I know it's not called Fart Mountain," Lucas tells her. "I told you that. I just think it's less scary if it has a dumb name."

"It is a dumb name," Dawn says. "Like, I can't even say it, it's so dumb."

"I know. That's the point." Lucas blows out a long stream of air. "Who told you it's called the Raven's Claw, anyway? Is that Warden's name for it?"

(The way he says *Warden,* Dawn can tell he's jealous.)

"He saw it on a map," Dawn tells him. "He said he stole the counselors' map and now he knows exactly where we are."

Lucas snorts and continues looking for firewood. "Stole."

"Yeah, stole. You know, like took without their knowledge?"

"Was that before or after he hooked up with her?" Lucas says without looking up.

Dawn stares at him. "What?"

"Amber," Lucas says. "You didn't know they're sleeping together?"

"Why would—when would they?" Dawn shakes her head. "That doesn't make sense."

Lucas shrugs. "You don't have to believe me," he says, continuing deeper into the forest. "Ask anyone. Why do you think Christian's so mad all the time?"

Dawn doesn't say anything.

"He's jealous," Lucas tells her. "He wants to get with Amber, but she has it for Warden, so he takes it out on everyone else. Plus, Kyla won't even look at him, no matter how many times he fails her, so . . ."

"He can't just be mean?" Dawn asks. "Why's it always got to come down to who likes each other?"

Lucas shrugs again. "Everything works that way," he says, reaching down to pick up another fallen branch. "Anyway, it got Warden a map, so who's really complaining?"

Something in Lucas's tone makes Dawn realize he's about done with the conversation, and that's just fine with her. She lets him wander off, and she heads back to camp with her armload of firewood.

Warden and Amber are nowhere to be found.

34.

IT'S ANOTHER LONG NIGHT.

This time, Dawn isn't worried about Fart Mountain/
Raven's Claw.

I mean, she is worried—tomorrow they're hiking to the
base of it—but she's mostly just thinking about Warden. And
Amber. And how Warden's hand felt in hers when he was saving her life up on that ravine. About the muscles in his arms
and the green of his eyes.

She's thinking about how strong he was when he pulled the
straps on her pack tight, how he nearly pulled her right on top
of him. She's thinking about how she maybe wouldn't have
minded being on top of Warden.

It's a long night.

Apart from her little brother, the men in Dawn's life are uni-
formly shitty.

She's never had a real boyfriend. She's dated a bunch of
weirdos and assholes, but, you know, that was more out of

boredom than anything else. It was more out of wanting to fit in, be normal. Normal girls date. So Dawn dated.

Meh.

And Julian is obviously bad news.

You knew that, though. He's a middle-aged bartender who smokes a lot of pot and can get Dawn into parties and whatever, but again, he's middle-aged and he's losing his hair and he always smells kind of funky.

(He's a middle-aged bartender.)

Plus he's always asking Dawn if she has any friends who'd be up for a threesome, and that shit gets old.

(Dawn doesn't have any friends.)

(Also, ewww.)

So anyway.

You know how you can go through your life never noticing someone until you go on a trip with them or have to do an assignment together and you more or less have to hang out for long periods of time and you start to realize that maybe you might actually have a thing for them?

(And sometimes it lasts past the end of the trip, and sometimes you get home and you wonder what the hell you were thinking, but that's kind of irrelevant right now.)

Yeah.

Dawn's in the middle of that stage, I think. Like, she's a total captive out here.

Warden is cute and brooding.

Lucas is cute and happy.

Where does it say that Dawn can't at least try to enjoy herself?

(Actually, it does say that. OUT OF THE WILD RULES AND REGULATIONS. Rule No. 6: No cohabitation between group members.)

(I.e., No hookups.)

(#Lame)

But rules are meant to be broken. And Dawn wouldn't even be here if she hadn't already proved she was willing to break a couple.

So with Warden in the picture and this burgeoning love triangle starting to heat up, let's take a minute to talk about Warden and Lucas and Dawn.

See, Dawn likes Lucas. Lucas is funny, and he's kind, and he's cute. He makes Dawn laugh a lot, and he makes the days go by quicker, and he's always around if Dawn needs help with something.

Lucas is a good guy. The world needs more people like him.

But Warden?

Warden is mysterious.

Warden is dangerous.

Warden is brooding and smoldering and sexy.

Warden is Dawn's kind of guy.

(Sorry, Lucas.)

35.

"I STOLE A TRUCK."

It's the next morning. Dawn can't look at Warden without blushing—or checking if Amber is in the vicinity—but here they are hiking together again. (Sorry, Lucas.)

The morning was the usual. Up at sunrise. Chores. Breakfast. Pack. Hike.

Blah, blah, blah.

They've left the lake and walked through the forest a short ways to another lake, which they've skirted around, and they're climbing through the trees again, but away from the ridge and up the other side of the valley, toward more cliffs and rocks and such.

Fart Mountain/Raven's Claw looms ahead. It's getting closer. It looks impossibly tall and, like, craggy. There still does not seem to be an optimal way to the top.

By the end of the day, the Bear Pack will make base camp at the bottom. By noon tomorrow, they'll be standing at the top. But Dawn's trying not to think about that. She's realizing she might actually be super afraid of heights.

She's trying to distract herself by asking Warden about his Origin Story.

―――――――

"I stole a truck," Warden says. "I stole it and I went on a little joyride and then I crashed it, and when I woke up in the hospital they told me I could either go to juvie or come here, so here I am."

He's from Oregon, he tells Dawn. Coos Bay.

"It's a shithole," he says. "There's nothing to do but get drunk and try not to fight surfers."

"You don't surf?" Dawn asks.

"Hell no." Warden gives her a look like he's personally affronted. "Surfers are douchebags. No exceptions. They take over the beach and everywhere else that's cool and if you're not part of their crew, you're like dog shit to them. You don't surf, do you?"

Dawn laughs. "I'm from Sacramento."

"Yeah, well," he says, continuing up the hill. "Good. Don't ever start."

They follow the rest of the Pack up a series of switchbacks until they're out of the trees again and looking across a wide bench of rock toward another far ridgeline. It juts out to their right, and in the distance lies the Raven's Claw. It looks incredibly close now, even though Dawn knows they still have nearly a full day's hike before they're even at the bottom.

"I guess it isn't so bad," Warden says, and it takes Dawn a moment to realize he's still talking about Oregon. "My mom's an ER nurse and she's busy all the time, so I can pretty well do what I want. It just sucks that everyone in town is either some douchebag surfer or a materialistic asshole."

"What about your dad?" Dawn asks.

Warden doesn't look back at her, but she can tell how his shoulders hunch up that it was the wrong thing to ask. "I don't want to talk about him," he says, and his voice is flat and dull. "He's not worth the effort."

"Okay," Dawn says. Warden doesn't say anything else, and they follow the trail toward the far ridgeline in silence.

Finally, near the top, Warden heaves a sigh, and his posture relaxes a little. "What about you?" he asks, glancing back at her. "What did you do to get stuck here?"

"Ran away," Dawn replies. She's half out of breath from the climb, so it's all she can manage. She's really hoping Warden doesn't look back again and see how gross and sweaty and out of shape she is.

But he does look back, his head cocked and his expression quizzical. He doesn't seem to notice she's gross.

"That's all?" he asks.

"I mean, habitually," Dawn says. She lets it sit a beat. "Plus, there was a little bit of a drug problem."

"Pot?"

"Pills."

"Nice," Warden says. "Your parents must have loved that."

Dawn forces a laugh. "Not even a little bit." She really isn't sure she wants to tell Warden about her dad. She doesn't say anything else.

"Why'd you run?" Warden asks once they're atop the ridge. "What was so bad that you couldn't stay home?"

Nothing, Dawn thinks. *Nothing was bad at home. Not until I fucked it all up.*

"I just don't get along with my stepdad," she tells Warden. "He didn't think I should be partying all the time. And I didn't think it mattered what he thought."

She's putting up a front, trying to sound brave and confident like she's all out of fucks, but it's pretty transparent, and Warden probably sees right through it.

He doesn't let on, though, doesn't push the point. "Parents suck," he concedes, and they leave it at that.

They hike for a while in silence. This ridge seems to lead straight to the bottom of the Raven's Claw, though you have to drop down into a deep, deep gulch and climb out the other side before you get there. The sun has come out and there's blue sky above them, and a beautiful lake down the ridge to their left. To their right, the ridge drops away into a wide, forested valley. There's still no sign of other people, just the trail and the occasional cairn, but today, with the sun shining, Dawn can actually appreciate the beauty—assuming she doesn't focus too intently on the mountain in front of them, tall and sharp and riddled with steep gullies were rockslides have ripped away at the face. There is *still* no obvious way to the top. Dawn's beginning to believe that Christian and Amber just intend to fake it.

"Where would you go, if you could be anywhere right now?" Warden breaks the silence. "I mean, judging by the look on your face, I'm guessing it's not up on *Fart Mountain*, right?"

"No, it is not." Dawn meets his eyes, grateful for the distraction. "I still can't believe we're going up there."

"It's not as bad as it looks." Warden shrugs. "I mean, I'm not saying it's easy, but we'll take it slow."

The way he says *we*, Dawn isn't sure he means the Bear Pack, or just the two of them. She kind of hopes it's the latter.

"I guess we'll see," she says.

"I promise, you'll be fine," he says. "I'll make sure."

He kind of smiles at her with those green eyes, and it's nearly enough to make Dawn believe him.

"So anyway, where?" he asks again, after the moment stretches a little too long. "Where would you go, if you didn't have to be here?"

Dawn hesitates. There's an easy answer for this; she's just not sure she wants to share it.

"Anywhere you want," Warden repeats. "Maui? Mount Everest?"

"Are those my two options?"

Warden rolls his eyes. "Come on."

Ugh, dude, Dawn thinks. *Quit making me share embarrassing shit.* But she plays the game anyway. Let him laugh if he wants to.

"Chicago," she says.

"Chicago."

Dawn meets his eyes. "My nana is there. My grandmother. I just wish I could see her again."

Warden doesn't laugh. He studies her. "When's the last time you saw her?"

"A couple years ago," Dawn says. "Usually we go visit her every summer, but this year, I . . ."

She trails off. Doesn't finish. Warden just watches her, and Dawn feels tears in her eyes. She bites her lip and turns away. "I can't stop thinking about, like, what if she dies while I'm out here," she tells the ridge and the lake and the valley—

(everything but Warden).

"What if she dies and I never get to see her again and it's all because I was too much of a freaking selfish bitch to go see her?"

Now the tears really are coming, and Dawn wipes them away, angry and embarrassed, and tries to stomp past Warden and continue along the ridge. But Warden puts his arm out, touches her shoulder, and it's gentler, not rough like when he fixed her straps yesterday.

"Hey," he says, and he waits until Dawn meets his eyes again. "You're going to see her again."

Dawn wipes her eyes again, hates herself and her stupid tear ducts. "I'm still a freaking Bear Cub, dude. I could be here until Christmas."

But Warden doesn't blink, those green eyes serious and concerned and really freaking pretty. "We're all getting out of here," he tells her. "You're going to see your nana again, I promise."

The way he says it?

Dawn actually kind of believes him.

36.

THEY MAKE BASE CAMP on the shore of a little glacial pond, literally in the shadow of, *ahem*, Fart Mountain.

Amber calls the pond a "tarn," but whatever that means, it's about the size of a swimming pool and the water is freezing cold. So is the air, for that matter; everyone bundles up in whatever they have in their packs, and they all sit by the fire wrapped in their sleeping bags when dinner is done.

The campsite is surrounded by gigantic boulders strewn everywhere. There aren't many trees at this elevation, just alpine grass and small, uh, *lichen* plants—thanks, Amber— clinging to the steep hillside. The Raven's Claw rises straight above them, reaching so high into the twilight sky you have to crane your neck almost straight up to see it. The summit is another half mile from where they're camped, and from here, the climb is mostly vertical.

"Hopefully the weather holds," Christian says. "It'll be a real pain in the ass if it snows while we're up there."

"It's not going to snow," Amber quickly assures them. "If

the last weather report is correct, we might see some rain tomorrow evening, but we'll be down from the summit by then."

She smiles at Dawn, reassuring. Dawn forces a smile back, even though she can't look at the counselor without wondering if Warden really is hooking up with her, and feeling kind of stupidly jealous about it.

Shut up, she tells her brain. *You have bigger problems right now. Tomorrow, you have to climb half a mile into the sky.*

Lucas keeps his distance tonight.

He's probably been watching Dawn and Warden hang out all day, and he's jealous, too. He might have even seen how Dawn started crying and Warden was there to comfort her.

Or maybe he's just tired, and as scared of climbing Fart Mountain as Dawn is.

Either way, he doesn't say anything to Dawn all evening. He hangs out with Alex instead, the two of them talking about sports and video games like they're overnight besties. He tries to make like he's ignoring Dawn, but Dawn knows better. He keeps stealing glances in her direction when he thinks she won't notice, but she does.

And when Dawn catches Lucas looking at her, he quickly looks away.

Morning comes early. Dawn wakes up from a dream that she can't remember except that Warden was in it and they were somewhere warm, and she was actually happy.

She wakes up shivering under her tarp just as the sky starts to get light again. It's been another restless, uncomfortable night.

Everybody moves slow but the counselors. Amber has a fire going already and water boiling for hot oatmeal. She gives Dawn a friendly look as Dawn crawls out of her sleeping bag. "Sleep okay?"

Dawn shrugs, mumbles something about coffee. Then she wanders off to find a boulder to pee behind.

While she's gone, all hell breaks loose.

37.

"MOTHER*FUCKER*!"

Kyla is screaming when Dawn comes back around the boulder, dreading having to wash her hands in the freezing-cold water of the tarn nearby. Kyla's voice makes Dawn forget about washing her hands.

Kyla is pissed.

"If you ever touch my ass again, dude, I swear, I will cut you," she's saying.

She's saying it to Christian, who is backing away from her with his hands up and his eyes wide, shaking his head and kind of laughing—like *Calm down, crazy; just relax*—and then he looks around and sees how everyone's watching him, watching what's happening, and he kind of goes a little bit red. "It was an accident, Kyla," he says. "Just chill."

But Kyla isn't having it.

"Yeah, an accident, bullshit," she tells him. "Just how many accidents are you going to have, asshole? You think I'm that stupid to fall for your shit?"

Christian glances around again, and nobody's turning away.

His face goes hard. His voice gets an edge to it. "Now, calm down," he says. "I apologized, and that's that. You keep making a big deal out of this, I'm going to have to—"

"Have to what?" Kyla asks. "Bust me back down to Black Bear so you can touch my ass for two more months?"

Christian starts to answer, but Kyla waves him off, turning back to her tent. "We all know what you're up to," she says. "Creep."

Christian claps his hands. "That's it, you're busted. Black Bear, Kyla. Congratulations."

Over her shoulder, Kyla shoots him the finger.

"Brown Bear, then."

She's singing now. "Fuuuuuuuck youuuuuuu."

"Bear Cub," Christian says. "I hope you like it out here."

For a beat, Kyla doesn't respond. Then she bends down by her tent, and Dawn thinks maybe she's just letting it slide, ignoring Christian, finally, like maybe if she just shuts her mouth he'll go away. But that's not what's happening here.

Kyla stands back straight, turning around as she does, and she's holding a huge, jagged rock, and her face is lined with tears.

"I fucking *hate* you!" she shrieks.

And she lunges at Christian with the rock. Pointy end first.

38.

"WHOA, *WHOA,* WHOA!"

Amber moves faster than Dawn's ever seen. In an instant, she's between Kyla and Christian, shunting Kyla backward, hugging her, holding her upright. "Whoa now," she says again, softer, like it's only for Kyla's ears. "Whoa now, let's all just relax, kay?"

Kyla's still glaring murder at Christian, her whole body shaking, still sobbing, but Amber doesn't let her go, doesn't stop talking, and Dawn watches as Kyla just, like, deflates, collapses limp in Amber's arms, dropping the rock with a thud and just breaking down, crying, the kind of crying you do when you're exhausted and broken and beaten and you just want to give up and, like, go die somewhere.

But Amber doesn't let go of her. Amber hugs her tight, and pets her hair, and Kyla lets her, still crying, and Dawn watches as Kyla's arms wrap around Amber, too, until they're hugging each other, hard, like neither one wants to let the other go.

And gradually Kyla stops crying.

Meanwhile, Christian is standing there like the piece of shit he so obviously is, watching Amber and Kyla with his lip curled like he wants to say something, but he doesn't, and anyway, it's doubtful his piece-of-shit language could permeate the barrier that Amber and Kyla have thrown up right now with their moment.

So Christian straightens and kicks a rock and glares around at the rest of the Pack. "All right, the show's over," he tells them. "Get packed up already. We move out in ten."

Dawn glances back at Amber and Kyla and thinks, *Fat chance.* Nobody else moves, either. Dawn watches Brandon and Evan exchange meaningful glances behind Christian. She feels her heart start to pound, though she isn't exactly sure why.

All she knows is Christian is suddenly very alone in the middle of the Bear Pack. And Brandon and Evan have looks on their faces like they know it, too.

The moment seems to hang there. Time seems to stop. Everyone's waiting to see what happens next.

Don't do it, Dawn mentally urges the boys, though there's a part of her that would like nothing more than to see Christian get his face kicked in.

Brandon and Evan study Christian for a beat. Then Brandon looks past the counselor and meets Warden's eyes, and it's like he's waiting to see what Warden thinks they should do.

And the rest of the group turns to look at Warden as well. *Don't do it,* Dawn thinks, and now she's mentally speaking to Warden, too. *Please.*

The moment stretches.

Brandon and Evan wait.

Then Warden's head tilts in a slight, barely perceptible shake. No.

And Brandon and Evan stare at Warden like they can't believe it, but Warden's expression doesn't change. Another long moment passes and then Evan shrugs, and Brandon shakes his head, and the spell is broken; the boys turn back to their tents and start packing, and time resumes its normal pace.

And Dawn lets out her breath, which she didn't even realize she was holding in the first place.

39.

"FIRST OF ALL, NOBODY'S GETTING BUSTED," Amber tells them all. "Christian and I have discussed what happened just now, and we're in agreement."

All eyes turn to Christian, who stands at the edge of the huddle and doesn't exactly look like he's in agreement with anything, but from Amber's tone of voice, it's clear there will be no negotiations.

"We're all tired," Amber continues. "We've got a big mountain to climb, literal and metaphorical, and I know that it's stressing us all out."

Kyla isn't looking at Christian. She's not looking at Christian in the way you don't look at someone when you want them to know they are the only fucking thing on your mind.

She's not looking at him, but she knows he's there. She's staring up at the mountain, her jaw set and her eyes clear, the tears on her cheeks wiped away, gone.

She looks tough and defiant. She's not looking at Christian, and it's a good thing, too, because if she were, he would probably burst into flames.

"Let's get through today," Amber is saying. "Together, as a Pack. Let's lean on our individual strengths and use them to help the team, and let's climb that mountain and get the hell out of here, and I promise Christian and I will pull some strings and we'll all have a nice meal and maybe a night indoors for once when we get back to headquarters."

Christian gives her a look, sharp. Amber cuts him down with one glance.

As for the rest of the Pack, shit, most of what Amber just said is psychological mumbo-jumbo, but getting to sleep inside doesn't exactly sound bad.

"What do you say, Pack?" Amber asks them. "Can we do this?"

There are halfhearted shrugs and maybe a couple of nods. Amber gives them a wry grin.

"I guess it's too much to ask for a cheer, huh?"

It's too much to ask.

"Well, all right, then," she says. "Let's send this bitch."

There are two routes to the top of the Raven's Claw that don't require harnesses and rope and other climbing gear.

"We're taking the scenic option," Christian announces, pointing to a ridgeline that runs left from the summit, an undulating spine to the top of the mountain.

"Are you sure?" Amber says, scratching her head. "We've never done it that way before. You don't think we should just stick to the tried and true?"

Christian shakes his head. You can tell he's just about taken his quota of L's for the day, and he's not about to give in easy.

"I was looking in the guidebook," he says. "The spine is supposed to be the same level of difficulty as the standard route. Anyway, it's like three hundred meters longer."

He looks around. "Longer means not as steep," he tells the Pack. "The other option is we go straight up the gut." He points to the right of the summit, where a series of rockslides has formed what looks like a sheer, slippery path to the summit.

"You said it yourself, we're all tired," Christian tells Amber. "We take the scenic route, we won't work as hard. Make the summit and get down fast before the weather kicks in."

Amber studies the mountain, her hands on her hips. You can tell she's not really into calling an audible at this stage of the game, but at the same time she's got to be aware she has totally undermined Christian's authority once already this morning—and the day is young—and she's got to at least *try* to present a united front of authority.

So Amber doesn't say anything.

"What do you guys think?" Christian asks the Pack. "You want to bust your asses up the gut? Or take it easy on the spine?"

There's a pause and a general murmur of not-wanting-to-answer and definitely-not-wanting-to-be-seen-agreeing-with-Christian, but mostly just shrugs and the occasional nod.

It's all Christian needs.

"That's what I thought," he says, turning left toward the spine. "Let's go."

This will turn out to be a BAD IDEA.

40.

AFTER ALL OF THAT CAMPSITE DRAMA, the day *truly* begins with a steady climb through a moderately steep alpine boulder field. The Pack plans to camp by the tarn again tonight, so they leave most of their belongings at the campsite. Christian and Amber bring daypacks with food and emergency supplies, and everyone in the Pack carries water and a couple of energy bars for snacks.

It's lighter going, but that doesn't seem to matter. Dawn is worn out and sweating through her shirt within ten minutes of leaving the campsite. The ground is slippery with loose rock and dewy lichen, and she can't find her footing and nearly twists her ankle a few times. Besides, her muscles are burning from just hiking to the base of this stupid mountain; she's not sure she has enough in the tank to make it up to the summit, and it's starting to scare her.

Lucas and Alex fall in beside her. "Crazy morning, huh?" Lucas says, panting for breath. "Christian's such a weirdo."

I guess it's friends-on again, Dawn thinks. "Did you see what happened?" she asks the boys. "I was peeing."

"I guess he touched that girl Kyla's ass, just like she said." Alex pulls himself over a boulder the size of a fridge. "It could have been an accident, but I don't really know."

Lucas helps Dawn over the same boulder. "Nah," he says. "I see no reason to doubt Kyla; Christian's done it before."

"He's a creep," Dawn agrees. She cranes her head toward the front of the Pack, high above, where Warden and Brandon and Evan are leading the way, climbing fast and steady with long, powerful strides.

Dawn has to tear herself away from watching how Warden's muscles ripple through his shirt, the way his triceps flex when he reaches to pull himself, the definition in his calves.

Down, girl.

"I think those guys are sick of it," she tells Lucas and Alex. "Like, if Amber hadn't stepped in, I don't know what would have happened."

Lucas and Alex follow her eyes to the boys at the front. Lucas frowns. "Those guys are bad news," he says. "Don't you think?"

Dawn shrugs. "We're all bad news, dude," she replies. "That's why we're here."

Alex laughs. "You guys don't seem so bad to me," he says. "All things considered. But that counselor—Christian? He's fucked."

Lucas makes to answer. Loses his footing on a patch of loose shale and slips and slides down about five or ten feet, ripping his pants, his palms coming up bloody. *"Shit,"* he says, the conversation forgotten. "I freaking *hate* Fart Mountain."

When they reach the spine it's like the sky opens up and they're standing on top of the world.

"You can almost see the ocean," Amber tells them, pointing in a direction that must be west. Dawn follows her gaze, but she can only see mountaintops and vast forest, same as always except more of it, miles and miles of unbroken wilderness.

Some of the mountains have snow on their peaks. The Raven's Claw doesn't, not yet. "Not the south face, where we're climbing," Amber tells Dawn. "It all melted away in the summer sun. But when we get to the top and you look down on the north side, I'm betting you'll see snow. That stuff lingers year-round. No sun to fall on it and melt it away."

At least I'm learning something, Dawn thinks. *Who knew kidnap and torture could be so educational?*

From their perch on the spine, the campsite down below looks tiny, the tarn barely the size of a postage stamp. And they haven't even climbed halfway to the summit yet. Ahead, the spine extends northeast, humping and rising along a thin, narrow crest, with sheer drops and gullies falling away on either side.

"Careful with this part," Christian calls back as he leads them onto the spine. "And if you have to fall off, fall to your right, so we can collect your body at the campsite when we come back tonight."

He grins back at them. It's not a nice grin. He motions to the north side of the mountain, where a long, steep glacier zone culminates in another perfect blue lake, a million miles from anywhere.

"You go that way, we're not coming to save you," Christian tells them. "That's helicopter territory, assuming you don't die outright from the fall."

The Pack just kind of stares at him, then at each other. Even Brandon and Evan look worried.

"I think I'm afraid of heights," Dawn tells Lucas.

Lucas nods back, grim. "Yeah," he says, looking up the narrow spine to the summit. "Me too."

$41.$

WHATEVER GUIDEBOOK Christian is reading, it's more fiction than fact.

They're halfway up the spine when it starts to get weird. Like the spine kind of, you know, truncates at this fifteen-foot-high wall that they're going to have to get on top of if they want to keep going, and that's fine and all, it's just fifteen feet up, BUT IT'S A THOUSAND FREAKING FEET DOWN IF THEY FALL.

(And if they fall the wrong way, even the rescue helicopters might not be able to retrieve their bodies.)

Terrifying.

Christian stops and kind of scratches his head and pulls out his guidebook. "Aha," he says. "We're just supposed to edge around to the north side of this wall. There's an easy chimney to climb over there."

The Pack looks at each other. They're strung out on this narrow spine with nothing but a steep, slippery drop on either side, and this motherfucker is talking about edging out onto the steep, slippery bits to climb up a chimney?

Even Amber looks worried.

"Christian," she says, "maybe we just call it, huh? Go back and try the normal way up."

"No time," Christian says. He's already edging out onto the top of the steep slope, kicking down rocks that go tumbling and tumbling for what seems like years, toward that pretty blue lake below. "We burned too many hours getting up here," he says. "If we want to summit this thing, we gotta go this way."

"So maybe we don't do it," Amber replies. "Climb back down, take a rest day, head for home in the morning."

Christian is unresponsive.

"Chris," Amber says. "We don't want to get anyone killed."

"No one's going to get killed." By this time, Christian has disappeared around the side of the wall, and his voice is barely audible over the, oh yeah, the chilly, high-altitude wind that is starting to pick up.

"Look," he says, "the chimney's right here. It's easy. We get over this and it's smooth sailing, I promise."

(Spoiler alert: it is not smooth sailing.)

First of all, just getting to the chimney is a nightmare. Dawn keeps slipping on the scree and sending it falling hundreds of feet down that, uh, approximately sixty-five-degree slope. And then the chimney is another form of hell.

It's steep and narrow and it's all loose rock that comes off in your hands as soon as you put your weight on it, or another person kicks it down at you as they make the climb, so you're always either ducking or holding on to something that feels like it's about half a second from crumbling and sending you falling to your inevitable death. And then there's the wind, which is still rising, and the fact that if you look down between your legs you can see the rest of the Pack clustered beneath you, waiting for you to get a move on, and beyond them that god-awful slope and the little blue lake far below, and it's enough to be freaking vertigo-inducing, panic-attack-causing, enough to make Dawn start to hyperventilate and freak out and freeze up on the mountain, which is exactly the kind of place you don't want to do those things, but all Dawn can think about is how she'll never see her nana again, and—

"Put your hand here."

(Huh?)

Dawn snaps back into focus. She's breathing hard and her whole body is shaking from being so scared. But when she looks up, there's Warden leaning down from the top of the chimney above her, pointing at a rock just above her head.

It looks solid. Dawn tries it. The rock holds her weight.

"Good," Warden says. "Now lift your right leg a little higher and there's a ledge you can sort of stand on."

Dawn does what he says, slowly, expecting at any second to pull the mountain down on top of her. Her foot finds the ledge. It holds.

"Right hand on that outcrop right there," Warden says. "Left leg beside your right."

Dawn hesitates.

"You got this," Warden tells her. "You're almost there. Just remember to breathe."

Dawn remembers to breathe. She listens to Warden. They climb the chimney together. And when she reaches the top, he's leaning down with his arm outstretched to pull her up the last couple of feet, and when Dawn gets to the top and out of that fucking chimney, she's so messed up and so grateful to be alive that she squeals and actually laughs and then she actually *kisses* Warden, just, like, spontaneous, and it's like an electric shock goes through her and she pulls back so suddenly she nearly falls back down the chimney—but Warden catches her.

"*Whoa*," he says, laughing and holding her steady. "Easy there, killer. We're not at the top yet."

He doesn't exactly look upset that she kissed him, though. Those green eyes are twinkling as he stares back at her, and he looks a little bit flushed himself, a little surprised and excited, and as they stand at the top of the chimney and wait for the others, Dawn wonders if Lucas saw her kiss Warden and if so, what he's thinking, and then she decides to push the thought from her mind and just really not care.

There's still a freaking mountain to climb after all.

The wind gets progressively stronger as they climb toward the summit. Eventually, the spine ends, and the Raven's Claw widens and steepens to almost vertical, and it's more chimneys and insane slopes and vertical views.

They take it slow, and Dawn and Warden work together, and Dawn doesn't have any more freak-outs, and slowly, but surely, they climb that stupid mountain.

And then they get to the ledge.

It's hard to be sure, from where the Pack is standing, but Dawn guesses they're only about a hundred feet from the top of the mountain. On the other side of the ledge, she can see where the trail curls up around some loose rock and keeps climbing, steep but not terrible, totally doable. The ledge, though, is going to be a problem.

The ledge is like two feet wide. There's a wall of rock on the right side, and lots of space on the left. Empty space.

Like, there's a fifty-foot drop and then just more scree and snow sloping down steeply all the way down the north slope of the Raven's Claw to that pretty blue lake in the middle of nowhere, the lake where even the helicopters will have to work hard to find you.

The wind is starting to howl now.

The ledge looks insane.

Christian's staring from the guidebook to the trail and back again, and you can almost see the words *OH SHIT* written on his face.

"Sweet," he says, trying to act like he hasn't just royally fucked them all over. "We traverse this here and then we're just about home free. Good work, guys."

His bullshit is totally transparent.

"I'm not crossing that," Kyla says, arms crossed. She's leaning against a slightly less sheer cliff as she takes a drink of water.

"Me either," Evan says. "This is freaking nuts."

Brandon nods in agreement.

Dawn looks at Warden, whose face is inscrutable. She looks at Lucas, who appears to be terrified. Alex looks from Christian to Amber like he's hoping common sense will prevail somehow; only Brielle doesn't look fazed, but she doesn't exactly look enthusiastic, either, from where she stands at the back of the Pack.

Amber nudges her way to the front. She surveys the ledge.

"Oh, man," she says, "I don't think we can do this, Chris."

Christian laughs. It sounds forced. "Of course we can," he says. "It's like a thirty-foot traverse, max."

"The drop is like fifty feet," Lucas says. *"Minimum."*

Christian ignores him. He's looking at Amber, who is staring at the narrow outcrop of rock her partner is proposing to, you know, *traverse,* and looking sick to her stomach.

(And when the Ambers in your group start to look scared, you know you're screwed.)

"Well, we can't turn back," Christian announces before Amber can say anything. "Those chimneys we climbed? Twice as dangerous going down as up. Best thing we can do is just tough this one out and then go down the easy way."

"The *easy* way?" Brandon says. "You said *this* was the easy way."

Christian huffs. "I meant the standard way." He looks at the Pack, one at a time.

(Even Kyla.)

"We'll take it slow, guys," he says. "Nice and easy. Don't

look down, and it's like walking on a sidewalk." Then, before anyone can mount another counterargument, he turns and starts walking.

Lucas gasps.

"Goddamn stupid idiot," Kyla mutters.

Amber reaches for Christian, but he's too far gone already. He hugs the rock on his right side, leans into it and presses his palms against the face, searching for cracks and handholds. Slowly, carefully, he makes his way across.

And then he's on the other side, arms raised, like *ta-da*, a big shit-eating grin on his face. "See?" he calls over. "Nothing to it."

"My ass," Kyla says. "I'm still not doing it."

But you know how guys are. As soon as Christian proves he can make it across, Warden and Brandon and Evan—and even Lucas and Alex—get this look on their faces like their manhood's in jeopardy if they don't also, you know, *send* the *traverse.*

So they do.

Warden goes first, obviously, and he looks better doing it than Christian by a mile, objectively and subjectively.

He makes the other side and there's no fanfare, no showing off. He just looks at Christian, hard, and then turns to look back across the ledge and shoots a cocky grin at Brandon and Evan.

"Come on over, ladies," he says—

(which is, ugh, not attractive, but w/e)

"Don't go soft on me now."

Brandon and Evan look at each other. They're practically shoving each other out of the way for the chance to go next, even though they're both obviously scared shitless and probably going to die.

Brandon wins, or loses, or whatever. He goes next. He goes slow. He hugs the wall tight, and his legs are shaking, and at one point he slips and kicks pebbles over the edge and Dawn hears them fall and thinks he's going next, like she's about to straight-up witness someone dying, but Brandon regains his balance and pauses to collect himself, and then he finishes the traverse like as fast as humanly possible.

Warden's waiting on the other side and he gives Brandon a pat on the back and a bro hug, and that's all Evan needs to go beetling across himself.

Alex takes a deep breath. Closes his eyes and psychs himself up. Then, calm and steady, he sends the traverse like a champ. Hits the other side and turns and looks back and smiles, kind of sheepish, at Dawn and the others.

Lucas looks at Kyla and Dawn and Brielle. "Uh, ladies first?"

The ladies all kind of look at each other.

On the other side, Warden and Brandon and Evan and Alex all yell encouragement.

(So does Christian, but nobody's listening to him.)

Dawn doesn't want to go next. She doesn't want to go at all, but that's probably not an option. But she's not ready yet.

Eventually, Brielle straightens. "I'll go," she says.

But Kyla either doesn't hear her or doesn't give a shit. She's shaking her head, muttering, positioning herself at the start of the ledge.

Inhale.

Exhale.

"*O-kay*," she says, shaking her head. "O-kay, this is *crazy*. This is really freaking *insane*." She looks ashen and shaky. Scared out of her mind.

But slowly—inch by inch—Kyla starts across.

42.

DAWN SNEAKS A LOOK at Amber.

She's expecting/hoping Amber will have some words of encouragement, something to tell Kyla and the rest of them that will make this whole ordeal go by easier.

But Amber's just pale.

Amber can barely watch.

Amber's got a look on her face like she just knows this is not going to end well.

And the shitty thing is . . .

                                                    Amber's right.

43.

KYLA HANDLES THE TRAVERSE like Wile E. Coyote handled running off cliffs in those old cartoons.

Which is to say, she gets like ten feet out and she's fine, and then she looks down and she's toast.

Unlike Wile E., though, she doesn't fall to her death.

She just, like, has a breakdown.

First, she freezes in place. Hugs the wall and tries not to look down again and looks down anyway, and then it's like in slow motion, she kind of collapses. She presses up against the wall and sinks down to her hands and knees, and Dawn can't see Kyla's face but she can tell she's sobbing.

Her whole body is shaking. Her head's down between her shoulders. She twists and tries to look back toward where Dawn and Amber et al. are watching, tries to maybe shuffle backward on her hands and knees, but it doesn't work so well. She shuffles a handful of loose stones right off the edge, and her left leg nearly slips off after them, and she screams and freezes in place again and just stays there, crying and shaking and refusing to move.

It's *no bueno*.

Warden is the first to react, on the opposite side. Smooth as can be, he picks his way to where the ledge begins, hunches down into a squat and looks like he's preparing to crawl out there to Kyla and get her.

"It's all good," he calls out to her, his voice barely audible over the wind. "You're all good, babe. I'm coming for you."

But he isn't, though. Because before he can make a move, Christian's behind him, his hands on Warden's shoulders, pulling him back, even as Warden tries to fight him off.

An argument ensues. Dawn can't make out what Christian is saying, but the gist is that Warden's not going back out there.

(You can imagine how Warden takes this news.)

Warden tries to push past Christian, and for a brief, heart-stopping moment, the guys are *wrestling* at the top of the cliff, and Brandon and Evan are watching, real close and edging closer like hyenas to a fresh kill, and Alex is trying to get between them and play peacemaker, and Dawn closes her eyes and looks away, thinking this can only end in disaster—and praying Warden isn't the one who dies.

But Warden doesn't die.

Neither does Christian.

Before the two guys can do anything really stupid, Amber blows the whistle on them. Like, literally. Somewhere in her safety kit she has a whistle and she digs it out and blows it like the world's highest-altitude referee, the piercing shriek even scaring the wind into momentary silence.

Christian and Warden stop cliff-wrestling. They kind of shove each other a little bit as they retreat to their corners, like guys do when they *really* want the other guy to know they're the alpha.

But they retreat anyway, and look across the chasm at Amber—who stares back, looking furious—and at Kyla, who is still frozen solid on that two-foot-wide ledge.

"You assholes just calm down!" Amber hollers across the void, and like the whistle before it, her words seem to mute even the wind. *"Stay there and don't move. I'll go to Kyla."*

Christian and Warden don't look at each other, but they nod.

(Nobody's messing with Amber right now.)

"Kyla, honey, you just stay put, too," Amber continues. *"I'll come to you and we'll do this together, kay?"*

Kyla shouts something back, but she doesn't have wind-silencing abilities at this juncture. Whatever she says, nobody can hear it.

Amber gives Dawn a reassuring smile as she turns back to the ledge. "Never trust a boy to do a woman's job," she says, winking.

Despite herself, Dawn smiles back. And then Amber's edging out along the ledge toward Kyla, saving the day yet again.

(Except this time, it doesn't work out that way.)

The whole Pack stops and stares as Amber inches out along the ledge toward where Kyla's still crouched on her hands and knees, trying not to have a total meltdown. Even Christian and Warden forget their beef and just watch. The wind picks up again, and Amber's words aren't loud enough for anyone but Kyla to hear, but Dawn can guess what the counselor is saying.

Just stay calm, honey. We got this. We'll get through it together.

Kyla's still shaking as Amber comes up behind her. Still crouched against the cliff face. Still kicking pebbles over the edge now and then; they bounce off the rocks beneath and scatter a hundred feet down in little clouds of dust.

It's just not a good scene.

Slowly, carefully, Amber makes her way to where Kyla's stalled, about fifteen feet from either end of the ledge. Amber doesn't look scared. Her face is drawn tight like she's concentrating hard, but she's only lightly touching the wall beside her for balance, and she moves smoothly, her knees bent but her head high, eyes always facing forward, never down.

(Amber is a freaking machine.)

(Dawn, on the other hand, is terrified for her.)

Amber reaches Kyla. She leans down and taps Kyla, lightly, on the back. Well, it's basically Kyla's butt, but nobody's raising a fuss about that now. Amber says something to Kyla. Kyla replies, shaking her head. *No.* Amber listens. Amber tries again.

The wind howls.

Amber and Kyla are out there for a long time. And every minute they're out there, the odds of a disaster happening get bigger and bigger. But Amber doesn't quit. She never looks nervous or anxious. She keeps talking to Kyla, coaching her, comforting her. And, eventually, she convinces Kyla to move a little bit forward.

Kyla moves, sobbing, an inch or two at most. But she doesn't fall. And from the look on Amber's face, you'd have thought Kyla just climbed Everest.

Amber keeps encouraging her. *You got this, girl. Take it slow.*

Kyla womans up and handles her business, little by little, one step at a time. She digs deep within herself and finds that inner courage and conquers the mountain and triumphs over fear and if this was a movie it's the part where the soundtrack would be soaring and everyone would be crying and even freaking Christian and Warden would hug it out because how could they not, right, when confronted with such a stirring victory of the human spirit?

If this was a movie, Amber wouldn't fall.

But it's not a movie.

44.

IT'S A FREAK THING, how it happens. Innocuous. It doesn't look like much until suddenly it's the Worst Possible Thing.

Kyla's almost at the end of the ledge. She's got her confidence back, moving faster. Maybe she's still crying, but she's laugh-crying, looking at Warden as he crouches down to meet her, saying something funny and encouraging and beckoning her forward.

We're all in this together. The whole gang's going to make it. Everything's right in the world.

Kyla gets overconfident. She gets sick of crawling. She's a couple of feet from safety when she stands up, suddenly and without warning, like she's getting off this freaking ledge on her feet, damn it.

Only problem is, nobody told Amber. And Amber's right behind Kyla, guiding her, encouraging her, and so when Kyla bolts upright like it's the hundred-yard dash, she brushes against Amber. She knocks Amber off-balance.

Time goes in slow motion.

Amber just seems to sway there. She sways there forever.

And if it weren't for how her face goes ghost white, you might not think there was anything wrong.

Ahead of Amber, Warden reaches out and grabs Kyla, pulls her to safety. Wraps her in a hug, and they're all too happy to notice how Amber's reaching behind her for the wall, trying to find an edge or a lip or a crack or something, anything, to find purchase and keep herself from falling.

But her hands only find smooth rock, and then it's too late. She looks straight at Dawn as she goes over the edge, and there's this look on her face and it's straight unfiltered fear. And then she's gone.

She doesn't scream, or if she does, it disappears into the wind.

She pinwheels in the air. Somersaults, her arms and legs flailing.

She drops fast.

She clears fifty feet in a blink, hits the steep slope at the base of the cliff, hits it awkward and sends up a huge cloud of dust and keeps falling, tumbling over sharp, bruising, body-breaking rock.

By now, Dawn is screaming. Kyla is screaming. Lucas is swearing very loudly. Warden is holding on to Kyla, trying to wrestle her into some kind of calm.

Christian looks ashen.

Amber keeps falling. Keeps rolling over rock, down, down, down toward the snow and the lake far below. She doesn't make it all the way, though. She slams into a boulder like half-way down, and just lies there.

She's too far away to tell if she's moving. She's just a green Gore-Tex speck against all that jagged gray. You can't see her face, or even really how she's situated. But it's obvious that she's probably dead.

The wind keeps roaring in Dawn's ears.

She keeps seeing Amber's face, right before she fell.

For a long time, that's all she can see.

It's Lucas who snaps Dawn out of it.

"We gotta get across," he says, shaking Dawn by the shoulders. "What if she's still alive? We gotta get her some help!"

She's not alive, Dawn thinks. *Weren't you paying attention? She fell like a mile, and she* bounced.

But Lucas isn't waiting for an answer. As Dawn watches, he crosses the narrow ledge quick and lithe, like a cat. Makes the other side with no problem and turns back and looks at her like he's surprised she hasn't moved yet.

Even Brielle's on the other side already. Everyone is waiting for Dawn.

Shit.

The rest of the Pack stands on the other side of the ledge and yells at Dawn to hurry up and get across, while at the same time they're stealing glances down the north side of the Raven's Claw, searching the snow and the rock for where Amber lies, broken.

Dawn tries not to look to her left.

(Don't look down.)

She tries to ignore her heartbeat and just focus on Warden and Lucas and Alex on the other side.

She closes her eyes and just runs.

And she makes it.

45.

NOW, THE WHOLE GROUP is together again.

And most of them crowd around Christian.

"What do we do?" Dawn asks the counselor. "You need to call for a rescue, right? You need to call back to headquarters *now.*"

Lucas and Alex and Brielle and Kyla are more or less saying the same thing. Brandon and Evan don't seem to give a shit; they're peering over the ledge toward Amber and kind of nudging each other and giggling about something.

Warden watches Christian like he's waiting to see what the counselor wants to do.

"Break out the radio, man," Lucas is saying. *"Make the call."*

Christian looks terrified. Like he's shitting bricks, like he's realizing Amber is dead and he's out of a job. And he's probably going to get sued.

He sets down his daypack and starts rooting inside.

Then he stops.

"Amber has the radio." He gestures over the edge. "It's down there."

Dawn wants to cry. The Pack's only competent counselor just fell, probably to her death, and she took the radio with her, and now they're all lost on top of this stupid mountain with no way to contact headquarters for help.

They're fucked.

They're so fucked that all Dawn wants to do is curl up in a little ball and cry until someone else solves the problem.

(And she almost does.)

But then she remembers.

"The rescue beacon," she tells Christian. "Where is it? Amber said you guys have the radio *and* a beacon. So where's the beacon?"

Christian blinks, like he's just waking up. He looks in his daypack again. The rest of the Pack watches him, waits.

Then Christian sighs.

"It's down at the tarn," he tells her. "I left— I forgot it. In my tent."

Dawn wants to shove him off the edge of the cliff. But there's no time. She turns to Lucas and Alex, about to enlist them to help her run down and find the beacon.

Call in the rescue helicopter.

Save the day.

But it's at exactly that moment that Dawn hears Alex gasp. He's staring down at the north slope toward Amber.

Pointing.

"Holy shit, guys," he tells the Pack. "She's *alive*."

46.

SHE'S ALIVE.

"She moved," Alex is saying, excited. "I swear to God, I saw her moving."

Dawn strains her eyes to stare down the north slope of the Raven's Claw to where Amber lies on that big boulder, a couple of hundred feet below. She fixes her stare on Amber's green Gore-Tex and tries to make out if Alex is telling the truth.

Dawn's eyesight is okay but it's not superhuman. She can still barely tell it's Amber down there. She's thinking Alex didn't see what he thought he did. Like, maybe the new guy got overexcited.

She's thinking there's no way Amber could survive that fall.

But then, as she's watching . . . Amber moves. It's not much, but it's unmistakable. Amber's green jacket shifts slightly. She raises one arm above her head and waves, just a little bit.

Just for a second or two.

Then her arm falls to her side again.

She stops moving.

There's no time to waste.

Lucas is already starting up the trail to the summit. "We gotta get down to camp," he tells the others. "Hit that beacon and hope they can send a chopper by nightfall."

Dawn's right behind him. Alex, too. Even Brandon and Evan are hauling ass.

Only Warden and Christian haven't moved. Christian's staring over the edge toward Amber, then back toward where the Pack is ready to move.

Christian looks scared. He looks *young*. He looks like he always knew he was coasting on Amber's competence and all-around boss status, and now that she's gone, he's got eight teenagers to keep safe and one gravely injured colleague to get rescued.

He looks like he's not really sure he's up for the job.

Fortunately, Warden seems like he's ready to fill the void. "You guys go," he tells Dawn. "Take the group down. Christian and I will stay up here and make sure Amber's okay."

Dawn looks at Christian, wondering how the counselor is taking Warden's little speech. To her surprise, he actually looks *relieved*.

Lucas tugs at her arm. "Come on, Dawn," he tells her. "Let's go."

Dawn glances back at Warden and Christian one more time. Then she turns and makes a break for the summit.

47.

THEY SAY THAT coming down a mountain is even tougher than climbing it. You expend so much energy on the climb that when it's time for the return trip you're running on fumes. You've already reached your goal, too, so now you just want to get back down to base camp, have a hot meal, climb in your tent. Celebrate.

You get tired. You get careless. You spent too much time on the come up, and now it's getting late and the weather's starting to turn. And just the technical *act* of descending is often tougher than the climb was in the first place. So people screw up. They lose focus. They get injured and die.

And that's in the *best* circumstances. Throw a wrench in the gears—like, I dunno, your only competent counselor falling, probably to her death—and it's bound to mess you up even more. The Bear Pack is in a hurry to get down the mountain to camp. Even Brandon and Evan, who don't give a shit about Amber, look like they're damn eager to get back to their tents.

But getting down isn't simple, even after they've covered the last hundred feet *up* to the summit. They'll take the standard route down, the route they should have come up, but it's not exactly a Sunday stroll.

It's basically a long drop down a sharp, narrow gully. There's a little bit of snow, but it's mostly loose, slippery rock and bare mountain underneath. Nothing to hold on to. Nothing to break your fall if you trip.

They take it as fast as they dare. Alex is in the lead, Brandon and Evan right behind him. Dawn barely notices who's ahead of her. She's mid-Pack with Lucas, trying to keep up, trying not to slide on her ass off the side of the mountain.

She can see the tarn where they camped last night. It still looks a long way down.

They drop through the gully, one after another, kicking pebbles and occasionally big rocks down toward the Pack members below them. Every now and then, somebody shouts, *"ROCK!"* and everyone has to duck as far off the trail as possible as a freaking boulder comes hurtling from on high, threatening to knock out or decapitate anyone in its path.

Miraculously, nobody gets hurt.

At the bottom of the gully, the mountain widens out to a broad, flatter shoulder, on which Dawn sees some lichen and a couple of cairns. This is obviously the way they should have gone: no chimneys, no ledges, no batshit traverses. They're still a long way from the bottom, but the really scary part is over.

The Pack hurries across the shoulder to the top of another gully. This one has a dry streambed cutting through the middle of it, all the way down to the tarn. It's not as steep as the gully above, and there are plants and the odd stunted tree. Still, it's easy to get careless, as Dawn discovers. She falls on a loose patch of earth and nearly takes out Lucas's legs ahead of her, probably almost killing them both. But Lucas stays upright and somehow arrests her slide. Looks back at her and grins, wearily, like *Ain't this some shit.*

And Dawn can't do much but shake her head in return.

This is hell.

"Come on," Lucas tells Dawn. "We gotta get down there before the weather turns."

He's not lying. It's probably about four in the afternoon at this point, which means it shouldn't be dark for another three hours, but already the skies are getting gloomier. To the west, Dawn can see storm clouds forming, rolling in over the distant peaks, getting closer. There's bad weather coming, and it's going to fuck up their day.

And if it storms too bad, Dawn thinks, *they might not even be able to bring in a helicopter.*

Dawn remembers what Amber said about the last weather report. *We might see some rain, but we'll be down off the summit by then.*

It doesn't feel like rain, though, the way the wind's biting, chilling Dawn through her jacket and numbing her face. Not at this time of year. Not this high in the mountains.

The wind feels like winter, from what Dawn can tell. And it's coming on pretty damn fast.

Alex gets back down to the campsite first. Brandon and Evan are hot on his trail. By the time Dawn comes out from the gully, she can see the three guys closing in on Christian's tent.

Behind her, the slope looks almost vertical from here. The peak of the Raven's Claw looks a mile high. Dawn can't even make out the summit; the whole side of the mountain just looks like sheer rock.

What she can see, though, is that the blue sky and warm sunshine the Pack was enjoying on their climb is now disappearing, replaced by ominous, swirling gray clouds.

The boys are almost at Christian's tent, and that makes Dawn hurry up, even though her knees are killing her by this point and she has blisters on her feet and her back hurts and she's tired as hell. Also, she's now walking through a boulder field, where the smallest rock underfoot is like the size of a soccer ball, and most are, like, fridge-sized, or even Volkswagen-sized. It's dangerous ground, lots of chasms to slip into and uneven ground to trip over. But somewhere, Dawn finds some last reserve of energy, some adrenaline she hasn't already wasted. She's struggling into the circle of tents just as Alex emerges from Christian's tent, holding the orange emergency beacon aloft.

She's almost caught up to Alex when Brandon and Evan tackle him to the ground.

48.

DAWN DOESN'T UNDERSTAND AT FIRST.

Brandon and Evan launch themselves into Alex, and they collide with the new Bear Cub and knock him backward into Christian's tent.

The orange emergency beacon goes flying, and Brandon bolts up and runs to it, picks it up as Evan stays on top of Alex, pinning him to the ground.

Dawn sees it happen, but it doesn't quite register.

Not until Brandon hurls the beacon into a rock.

No, Dawn thinks, feeling paralyzed and suddenly sick. *No, Brandon, what the hell are you doing?*

The beacon explodes against the rock. Clatters to the ground as Dawn and Lucas watch, incredulous—

(and Brielle and Kyla pick their way into camp behind them)

(and Alex struggles underneath Evan, who still has him pinned)

—as Brandon walks to where the beacon landed.

He kneels down.

He picks up a nearby rock, about the size of a grapefruit.

And slowly, methodically, he begins to pound the beacon
into tiny, useless pieces.

49.

DAWN SCREAMS, *"What the fuck are you doing?"*

She runs across the uneven ground past Christian's tent and Alex and Evan to where Brandon stands, triumphant, over the useless wreck of the beacon.

She kneels down amid the rocks and picks up what's left of it, and the beacon is in pieces and the pieces are small, and it will never, ever make an emergency call again.

She stares at the pieces.

Lets them fall from her hands.

Feels suddenly very cold, and it has nothing to do with the storm blowing in.

She stands up slowly and turns around to see Alex shove Evan off from on top of him. Watches the new guy push himself to his feet, wincing.

Brandon and Evan just stand there with smirks on their faces. Lucas and Brielle and Kyla stare back, disbelieving.

"What the fuck, Brandon?" Kyla says after a beat. "Have you gone completely insane?"

"How are we supposed to call the rescuers?" Dawn asks. "Dude, what the *fuck?*"

Brandon's expression doesn't waver. "We're not going to call the rescuers," he says.

Dawn blinks. Feels like she's in an alternate dimension where nothing in life has to make sense. "Why not?"

Evan sniggers. "Because they're not freaking rescuers, dumbass. They're prison guards, just like Amber and Christian."

"Amber isn't a prison guard," Dawn says.

Brandon rolls his eyes. "Weren't you kidnapped?" he asks her. "Do you actually want to be here?"

"Fucking *nerd*," Evan mutters.

"This is our chance to get away," Brandon tells her. Tells all of them. "Why the *fuck* would we call in more counselors?"

Dawn stares at them. Still trying to process. "So, what? You're just going to leave Christian up there? And *Warden?*"

And Amber, she thinks, but she already knows that Brandon and Evan don't give a shit about Amber.

Brandon and Evan swap glances.

"Christian, maybe," Evan says.

"Not Warden," Brandon says.

He gestures with his chin back toward the Raven's Claw.

As one, the rest of the Pack turns.

And watches as Warden picks his way out of the gully. And comes walking across the boulder field toward them.

50.

WARDEN DOESN'T SAY ANYTHING until he reaches the middle of the campsite. Until he's sure the whole Pack is looking at him: Brandon and Evan standing by the remains of Christian's tent. Dawn by the wreckage of the emergency beacon. Alex wiping blood from his mouth. Lucas and Kyla and Brielle just kind of watching him, agape.

Then he surveys the group, meets their eyes. Kind of chuckles.

"Well, hey," he says, grinning. "I guess we'd better have a team meeting."

They adjourn, uneasily, to the remains of last night's fire. They stand in a circle, and they all watch Warden.

"Brandon's right," Warden tells them. "There's no rescue. There's only going back to the way things were before. If we want to be *really* rescued, we have to do it ourselves."

Dawn looks around at the other group members. Alex looks angry and confused. Lucas about the same. Brielle's expression is inscrutable, but she never takes her eyes off Warden. Kyla, though, looks like she's starting to hear Warden. She's inched a little bit closer to where he and Brandon and Evan stand.

"But what about Christian?" Dawn asks. "What about *Amber*?"

"Christian's still up at the summit," Warden says. "In a couple of days, when we don't show up at headquarters, someone will send a rescue team looking for us." He looks at Dawn. "We don't even know if Amber's still alive by now," he says. "We can't waste this opportunity we've been given."

"So, what?" Lucas asks. "What are you suggesting we do?"

"I'm suggesting we get the hell out of here," Warden replies. "We can hike it. I remember from the map, there's a way out of here, around the backside of the Raven's Claw. There's a highway, like, twenty miles north."

Kyla groans. "Twenty *miles*?"

"It's not hard," Warden says. "We just follow a river. We've got enough food to make it, and we'll have a couple days' head start on whoever comes looking for us."

"And then what?" Dawn asks. "Are we supposed to just, like, hitchhike back home?"

Warden sighs, like the way your teacher sighs when you're just not *getting* a concept. "You need to stop thinking about this as just a speed bump on the way back to normal," he tells her. "If we get out of these woods, Dawn, we're not *going* home."

Dawn doesn't say anything. Her head's spinning.

Warden looks at Kyla.

"Kyla, when we get out of here, you never have to worry

about your mom's stupid boyfriend again, or the judge who sent you. Just go off and do something new; whatever you want."

He turns to Lucas. "Bro, you can forget about the army, or whatever your dad wants. Make your own life. Fucking take control, right?"

Lucas nods, though it's clear the idea of telling his dad to fuck off kind of terrifies him.

"Alex, you're new, and, Brielle, you hardly ever speak, so I don't really know either of you, but once we get out of here, you can do whatever it is you want to do," Warden says. "And, Brandon and Evan? You guys can, shit, I don't know. Give each other handjobs in a truck stop bathroom or something, whatever you're into."

Nearly everyone laughs. Even Brandon and Evan, though Dawn notices they refuse to look at each other.

Then Warden turns to Dawn. "Dawn," he says, "listen. You want to see your nana, right? Wouldn't you rather be in Chicago than here?"

Dawn doesn't answer.

"We can go to Chicago," he says.

Brandon and/or Evan makes an *ooooh* noise like Warden just told Dawn he has, like, a crush on her.

Warden shoots them the finger. "Not like that, assholes," he says. "Just, like, we'll hitchhike, or something. Scrounge up money for the Greyhound. We'll go to Chicago. You can visit your nana. Isn't that better than just going home?"

It is better.

It's so much better.

Warden has her, and he knows it.

Dawn wants to see her nana so bad it nearly makes her cry to think about it, and now that Warden's mentioned how the Out of the Wild people will probably get them in trouble once they figure out what happened here—

> (and let's be real, it would *totally* not be beyond Christian to try to rewrite history and blame the Bear Pack for what happened)

> > —well, Dawn isn't sure she'll ever get out of this program.

> > > (Or, like, *jail.*)

She doesn't want to go home to her mom and her stepdad. She doesn't want to go home to Julian. She wants to see her nana. And Warden looks so sure of himself, so confident he can lead them out of here, that Dawn starts to believe in his plan.

She starts to believe he can lead them twenty miles through the mountains and out to the highway. That he can take them from the highway to somewhere they can all scatter, disappear across the country like ghosts.

That he can take her to Chicago. To Nana.

Dawn starts to believe this is What Happens Next.

"I just need you to trust me," Warden says. "Do you trust me?"

51.

"NAH," ALEX SAYS.

Dawn blinks, turns to look at him, realizing she almost forgot the rest of the group is here. Like she's been lost in Warden's green eyes for a minute or two, and it's only the sound of the new guy's voice that snaps her out of it.

The Pack turns to look at Alex, who shrugs.

"No offense, dude," he tells Warden. "I'm sure you know what you're doing and you can get these folks to the highway. I just don't really feel the need to escape."

Warden says nothing. Just stares at him.

"It's like," Alex says, "that counselor, Amber, she might still be alive. And we all know Christian doesn't know what he's doing. You all do your thing; I'll hike back to headquarters on my own. Call in the rescue chopper and I'll play the hero.

"Shit," he says, grinning. "They might even let me out early."

For a long moment, nobody says anything.

Brandon and Evan look at Warden, as if they're waiting on his cue for how to react. Dawn realizes she's waiting, too. And she's seeing how Alex doing hero things will get her off the hook—like, she doesn't have to feel guilty about abandoning Amber. Not if Alex stays behind to shoulder that burden.

She can skip out with Warden and make tracks for Chicago.

She can leave her old life in the dust.

After a beat, Warden nods.

"Yeah," he tells Alex. "Okay. You head back to headquarters, make sure the rescue team can find Amber. Just don't tell the prison guards where we're headed."

Alex makes a gesture like he's zipping his lips. "Snitches get stitches," he says. "I won't tell."

It's at that moment the wind suddenly picks up, and the first drops of rain blow in hard and cold from the west. Above the campsite, the Raven's Claw is now completely obscured by clouds; the day's light is waning, and the storm's getting closer.

Dawn shivers.

"There's no point in leaving tonight," Warden tells the Pack. "We're better off making camp before this weather gets worse. Get a fire going, get dinner started. We need to work as a team."

Warden's eyes are on her, and Dawn realizes he's looking for allies.

We all need to work as a team.

She claps her hands, feeling suddenly energized. "I'll gather firewood," she announces. "Who wants to start pumping water?"

AUTHOR'S NOTE

IT COULD BE THAT at *this point you're thinking Dawn's plan is a little unrealistic.*

Like, surely she can see that her nana will call Wendy and Cam the minute Dawn shows up in Chicago, and Dawn will get her ass hauled back home.

This is true.

And Dawn knows it's a possibility.

But she also knows:

1) She *really* wants to get off this mountain, and
2) She can *probably* convince her nana to hold the phone on calling Cam and Wendy, for a couple of days, anyway. At least long enough to try to explain why her nana shouldn't just send her back.

Also:

3) She REALLY wants to get off this mountain.

She'll figure out the rest when they get to Chicago.

52.

TEAMWORK MAKES THE DREAM WORK. Or at the very least, it keeps you and your besties from freezing to death.

It's tough to find firewood up here in the alpine. The trees are all stunted and small, and there isn't much dead wood just lying around. Dawn has to go pretty far out from the campsite to find anything good, down along the trail they followed to get up here. Brandon and Evan are getting firewood, too; she can hear them laughing and jostling each other somewhere nearby, but she never quite sees them.

It weirds her out, though, how, like, *unaffected* they are by this whole turn of events. Like, Amber might die. There's a big storm coming in. The radio's smashed, and their first thought was to destroy the emergency beacon.

Even if it means Amber might *die*.

It's getting dark now. Cold. Dawn walks so far down the trail that all she can hear is the wind and the boys' disembodied laughter. There's not much of a trail, either, and when there is, it seems to branch off in a bunch of directions. Dawn is so focused on finding wood that she's hardly paying attention anymore, and soon she can't even hear Brandon and Evan.

Dawn looks up with an armload of firewood, and she can't remember which way she came from.

Around her, a few flakes of snow start to fall, and suddenly, Dawn realizes she's lost. She's been following a path that she thought was the trail going back up to camp, but it veered off and terminated at the edge of a cliff. If it had been any darker, Dawn might have walked off it.

"Damn it."

She left her headlamp behind, too, like a rookie. Like a Bear Cub. And pretty soon it will be too dark to even make out the ground.

Dawn stands there, dumb, her brain starting to panic. Her heart starting to pound and her thoughts yelling at her.

You can't just stand here.

There's no time.

You'll die in the dark if you don't find the trail.

MAKE A DECISION.

It's too much. It's overwhelming. Dawn is tired and she's hungry and she's emotionally spent. She climbed the Raven's Claw today, to the top, the hard way. She watched Amber plummet to the bottom. She climbed back down again. She needs food and warm clothes and a sleeping bag.

She's exhausted, and it's all catching up to her now.

Shit.

"Hey."

A voice startles her out of the impending panic attack. It's a girl's voice, and since it's not Kyla, it has to be Brielle.

"Brielle?" Dawn says, ashamed of how small and childish her voice sounds. "Where are you?"

A headlamp blinks through the patchy trees, and Dawn can see Brielle approaching, little more than a silhouette in the dying light. Brielle closes the distance quickly; she's small and graceful and agile, and she doesn't appear at all overwhelmed or exhausted.

"Lost?" she asks Dawn.

Dawn nods. "I was just about to freak out."

"Don't do that," Brielle says. She gestures at Dawn's arms. "We need your wood." Then she cocks her head. "That's what she said."

Dawn laughs, despite herself. Holds up the branches she's been collecting. "I've got enough wood for everyone."

Brielle smiles at her. It's a weary smile, but it's a friendly one. "Then I guess you're my new BFF," she says. "Let's get back to camp."

53.

"THIS IS FUCKED UP, RIGHT?" Dawn asks Brielle, as she follows the smaller girl up toward the boulder field, the tarn, and the camp. "I mean, this whole thing is psycho, isn't it?"

Brielle turns, the light from her headlamp cutting a swath through the dark night. They're up in the alpine again, and the beam finds nothing but open air before it peters out into shadow. Dawn knows they're in wide-open space, but she still feels claustrophobic, suffocated by the darkness. It's an eerie, unsettling feeling, being out here like this.

"Which part?" Brielle asks. "The part where our counselor just fell off a cliff? Or, like, in general terms how we're enduring forced marches that are definitely *not safe* because our parents and/or parole officers think we could all use a little fresh air?"

"I don't even know how this is legal," Dawn agrees. "Like, Christian is completely unqualified to be out here."

"And he's a freaking child molester."

"That, too," Dawn says. "But I guess I meant more about Brandon and Evan."

Brielle keeps walking. The trail is steeper now, gaps between the rocks.

"Yeah," she says quietly. "That *is* fucked up."

"You think Amber will make it?"

"I dunno. Depends if Alex can get back to headquarters in time." She pauses. "Depends if they let him."

Dawn waits, but Brielle doesn't elaborate. "Who?" she asks. "Who's going to let him do what?"

"The boys," Brielle says. She lets it sit there a beat, like Dawn should understand. Then, when it's clear Dawn doesn't, she sighs. "He's kind of throwing a wrench in their plans. Don't you think?"

"What do you mean?" Dawn suddenly feels like the girl who walked into AP Japanese and can't even pronounce *konnichiwa*. "What are you talking about?"

They come up over a rise, and suddenly Dawn sees more light: flashlights, and the glow of a fire, closer than she expected.

A flashlight turns in their direction. "*There* you are," Warden says, climbing over the rocks toward them. "Jeez, I was starting to get worried."

He ignores Brielle, walks right past her and puts his arm around Dawn and takes the wood from her. "Come on," he says. "Kyla's almost got dinner ready."

Dawn lets Warden take the branches from her. Hangs back

as she follows him into camp, hoping to get an answer from Brielle.

But Brielle is gone, she realizes. The Black Bear has slipped off and disappeared again, leaving Dawn with nothing but more questions, and the sick feeling that more bad things are coming, just as sure as the storm is.

54.

IT'S NOT UNTIL SHE'S ACTUALLY EATING that Dawn realizes how hungry she is.

She's starving.

She hasn't eaten anything but energy bars since breakfast, and with the whole stress of the day and Amber falling and then the getting-lost-in-the-dark thing, Dawn's been too distracted to eat.

But now, as she stirs her spork into one of Christian's emergency dehydrated mountain-climber mystery-meat dinners, Dawn can hear her stomach growl and feels a little dizzy, and even the mystery meat looks like prime rib.

It's actually some kind of pasta, according to the package. All Dawn knows is that it's hot and it's filling and it's better than energy bars or, like, the sack of rice she's been lugging around since forever.

It's freaking delicious.

She eats so fast she doesn't realize Warden's watching her, but then she looks up from the little tinfoil bag and catches the gleam in Warden's eyes across the campfire and it's obvious he's been looking at her pigging out this whole time, and Dawn sits up straighter and puts the bag down and tries to swallow and smile back and look cool without, you know, making a fool of herself, and then Warden makes a gesture like he's wiping his chin and his smile never wavers and Dawn sets her spork down and touches her own chin and there's like, drool or pasta sauce all over her face, and Warden bursts out laughing and Dawn spins away, mortified, but she kind of has to laugh, too, and on the other side of the fire, Lucas makes a disgusted noise and looks away.

And Warden's still watching Dawn, and his eyes are still alight with the glow of the fire.

"What about Christian?" Dawn asks as the wind continues to pick up around the fire circle.

Brandon and Evan kind of snicker. "What *about* Christian?" Evan says.

But Lucas gets it. "He doesn't have a tent up there at the summit," he says. "The way this storm's blowing in, shouldn't we be worried? Like, it's bound to be pretty cold up there over-night."

Dawn glances at him, grateful, but Lucas ignores her. He's watching Warden instead. So is everyone else.

Warden shakes his head. "We found a cavern up there," he says. "Just, like, a little sheltered overhang. And Christian had an emergency blanket in his bag; I made sure of it. He'll be cold tonight, but he should be okay."

He looks at each group member in turn, and he sounds confident and not worried at all.

And Dawn figures that means she doesn't need to worry either.

<hr />

Night falls around them. The wind's blowing hard now, whipping the flames from the campfire to and fro, sending sparks billowing up skyward in clouds of light. It's *cold* now, away from the campfire, and Dawn can feel the first drops of rain on her face.

Shit, she realizes. *I haven't even set up my tarp yet.*

She stands up from the fire circle into a bitter blast of wind, already hating the thought of setting up her stupid tarp in the dark before it starts to rain too hard. Knowing she'll never stay dry enough, warm enough, to get any sleep tonight.

You should have picked the tent, she tells herself. *Not the goddamn backpack.*

It's going to be a long, awful night.

55.

"WHAT ARE YOU DOING?" Warden asks Dawn as she fumbles around in the dark for her pack.

"My pack," Dawn tells him, shining her flashlight across the ground. She's sure she left it right here. "I still have to set up my tarp for the night."

Warden appears out of the gloom, stretching lazily, his hoodie riding up to reveal his flat stomach, toned abs. "Oh, you won't need your tarp," he says.

Dawn looks at him like he's crazy, and Warden shrugs. "It's going to drop below freezing tonight," he says. "You don't want to catch hypothermia, do you?"

"Of course not," Dawn says. She starts to tell Warden that she has to sleep under her tarp, it's the rules, but she stops herself just in time.

"I have to sleep somewhere," she says.

"You can share my tent." This isn't Warden. It's Lucas. He comes out of the dark on the other side of Dawn and shrugs and tries to look nonchalant. "I have a big tent. There's plenty of room."

Before Dawn can answer, Warden shakes his head. "That's cool of you, man, but I already moved her stuff into my tent. I've got lots of room, too."

He looks at her. "I'm not trying to hit on you," he says. "It's just you've got to stay warm and dry at this altitude. Especially with the storm coming in."

Lucas looks like he wants to argue. Say something. But what is there to say?

(Anyway, Warden cuts him off at the knees.)

"Thanks, man," he tells Lucas. "Looks like we've got the situation taken care of."

(Sorry, Lucas.)

It's not the *best* feeling in the world, being caught between the two guys like Dawn is.

Feeling like no matter what she does, she's going to hurt someone's feelings.

And suspecting that it's going to be Lucas she hurts.

"You know what, it's fine," she says. "I'll just sleep in Christian's tent. It's not totally fucked up from Alex and Evan, right?"

But Lucas is already turning to leave.

"Christian's tent is ruined," he says. "Go ahead, crash with Warden." He pauses. "Or don't. It doesn't matter to me."

Dawn hurries to follow him. "Lucas."

"What?" He spins. "You think I don't know what's going on here, Dawn? You and Warden?"

Dawn glances back to where Warden's watching them, fifteen or maybe twenty feet away. "It's not like that," she hisses.

Lucas laughs but there's no funny in it. "Oh yeah?" he says. "Then why did you *kiss* him, Dawn?"

Dawn opens her mouth, but she doesn't say anything.

"I thought we had something cool," Lucas says. "I thought we, you know, liked each other."

"We do," Dawn says. "I do. I just—"

"You just like Warden more." Lucas shakes his head, bitterly. Then he starts to walk away from her again. "It's fine, Dawn. No worries. Have a good night."

He disappears into the darkness, and Dawn watches after him. Wants to say something, but there's nothing to say.

She's too tired for this drama, anyhow.

<hr />

Warden's sitting by the fire when Dawn comes back from her little tiff with Lucas.

He's alone.

Dawn can see light in the other tents spread around the campfire; she can hear rustling as the rest of the Bear Pack gets comfortable for the night. But Warden's just sitting there watching the fire die, his hoodie up over his head and the flames dancing in his eyes.

"Everything okay?" he asks, smiling that mischievous smile as Dawn comes back into the circle, like he knows what's going on between Lucas and Dawn, and he knows how Dawn's conflicted about it.

Dawn tries not to blush, avoids Warden's eyes. "Everything's cool," she tells him. "Look, I think I'll just crash with Kyla or something. Save everybody the trouble."

Warden nods. "Lucas is upset," he says. "Jealous."

"I guess so," Dawn says.

"He has a thing for you."

Dawn shrugs.

Warden stands and walks to his tent. Unzips the flap and shines his light inside.

"Look, it doesn't have to be like *that*," he tells her. "You can crash in here and we can be good, I promise. I just didn't want you to sleep in the cold."

He sounds so innocent when he says it that she almost believes him, and his eyes are clear of the mischief that often lives there.

(Dawn isn't sure if she *wants* to believe him, but that's a different thing entirely.)

"But hey," Warden says, "if it's a big deal between you and Lucas, believe me, no worries." He reaches into his tent and comes out with her backpack. "The last thing I want is to fuck up group dynamics."

He hoists her pack and makes to hand it across to Dawn. Dawn stares at it. At Warden behind it. And she's suddenly aware of how cold she is already, and wet; she's shivering and her teeth are chattering and her toes are like ice, her pants wet and her legs wet underneath them and her feet are the worst of all, and she's suddenly aware of how nice it would be to get warm and cozy and curl up beside somebody and not just, you know, shiver the night away by herself, and she must be sub-consciously looking inside Warden's tent, because he seems to read her mind.

"We can be good, I promise," he says. The way he smirks makes Dawn feel like she's being childish. "It doesn't have to be anything you don't want it to be."

Dawn hesitates.

She closes her eyes.

She wonders how she's going to face Lucas in the morning.

But then she takes her backpack from Warden and puts it back in his tent.

> (Hell, she was probably going to fall
> for Warden at some point anyway.)

56.

CHANGING IS A CHORE.

Changing clothes in a tent is hard enough as it is. Changing clothes in a sleeping bag is worse. Changing clothes in a sleeping bag when you're shoulder to shoulder with a guy you kind of like?

Impossible.

"I won't look," Warden tells her. "I promise."

Somehow, Dawn pulls it off. She shimmies out of her wet clothes while somehow still remaining covered by the sleeping bag, and she pulls on dry undies and pants and a fresh T-shirt and socks, and she zips up her yellow Bear Cub fleece. She wads up her wet pants and her stinky socks and pushes them down to the very bottom of her pack, and then she pushes her pack down to the far end of the tent by her feet, and she lies back down again and pulls the sleeping bag over her shoulders and up to her neck and she's still cold and still kind of shivering, but at last she's starting to get warm, and starting to get comfortable, and maybe in a while, *maybe*, she'll actually be able to relax.

It's cozy in Warden's tent, that's for sure.

It's a double tent, but just barely; Warden's so tall that he kind of sleeps at an angle, and the tent isn't even that wide. As soon as Dawn slides into her sleeping bag she can feel him beside her, pressed close, even through two layers of sleeping bag material, and it's nice to be warm and it's nice to be dry, and it's nice to be this close to somebody.

(Sorry, Lucas.)

57.

THEY LIE THERE IN SILENCE.

Dawn and Warden.

Warden and Dawn.

At some point, Warden turns off his flashlight, and the tent is pitch dark, and all of a sudden Dawn is hyperaware of the sound of the wind gusting against the tent, and the sound of the rain falling against the tent.

And the sound of Warden's breathing.

And the sound of her own.

She can't see Warden, and she doesn't know what he's doing; she can feel him next to her, some warm amorphous blob, but she doesn't know where he's facing or whether his eyes are open, and she sure as hell doesn't know what he's thinking.

But then he shifts in his sleeping bag and she can feel his breath, warm, and she knows he's sitting up, slightly, and looking her way.

"So," he says, and she can hear the mischief, hear the smile in his voice. "Are you sure you want to be good?"

She's felt this way before.

That hollow oh shit *feeling, like you're suddenly falling.*

Like the ground you've been standing on has suddenly dropped away.

Like you've been ambushed, straight out of the blue, and now you have a decision to make, and neither answer is easy.

Do you:

    a)   *Play along and be fun even though you're not sure, or*

    b)   *Resist and be awkward and probably blow your shot?*

Dawn has been here before.

It was Julian last time.

It was Julian and they were standing in the parking lot outside some club, and Dawn didn't know him yet but he said he had pills to share, so she'd gotten her hand stamped and followed him out, and he'd led her through the lot and around back of the club and into an alcove, an emergency exit near, like, a dumpster and probably hundreds of rats.

And he *did* have a stash—he showed her, he had plenty— and he swore it was good shit, but the way he looked at her,

Dawn could tell he wanted something and it wasn't money, even though she kept offering to pay him for it.

But it wasn't just that—like, it wasn't just *transactional.*

Julian was cute, in the lights of the club, in a *Sons of Anarchy* dirtbag kind of way. And Dawn was in one of those moods where no matter how many vodka sodas you drink it's still not chasing the demons from inside your head and you just really need something stronger.

But it was cold in the parking lot, and the alley was deserted. And in the harsh light from the streetlights and security lights, Dawn could see that Julian wasn't just old, he was, you know, *old.* Like, way too old to be even talking to Dawn, let alone plying her with illicit substances.

And she could see how the *Sons of Anarchy* dirtbag look wasn't just some hipster disguise.

But somehow, Dawn still wanted to impress him. She didn't want to be the lame chick who didn't play along, who chickened out at the last second.

She stared at Julian, suddenly far too uncomfortably sober, and she studied the gleam in his eyes and tried to imagine just how far he would want to go, and how she could mitigate this suddenly far too uncomfortable situation.

And Julian grinned back, like he had all day, like it didn't matter to him either way, but she sure as hell wasn't getting high on his shit without paying a price for it.

You know what happened.

58.

BUT THIS IS DIFFERENT.

"I think I want to be good," Dawn says. "I'm sorry."

(Because Dawn knows you always have to, like, *apologize*, if you're a girl and you're not sure you want to do what a boy wants you to do.)

And Dawn can almost *hear* the disbelief spread all over Warden's expression, hear the deafening echo as his eyes blink in shock and he realizes this girl who clearly likes him and who's alone in a tent with him as a storm kicks up outside, this girl who he thought was a sure thing . . .

This sure thing isn't exactly so sure.

And Dawn knows Warden isn't really the type to have to deal with rejection too much. Not with those eyes and those abs.

She wonders if she should have just opted for the tarp. And hypothermia.

Warden kind of stiffens and waits there a beat, and then he

backs off and lies down and lets out a puff of air. "Okay," he says. "Suit yourself."

"I'm sorry," Dawn says again, but Warden doesn't tell her it's okay, or that she has no reason to be sorry.

He just puffs out another long puff of air. "Good night."

59.

DAWN LIES AWAKE.

Warden is snoring within a couple of minutes, because of course he falls asleep quickly, because he's a guy and he doesn't have to worry that he's somehow screwed everything up just by not wanting to fool around.

(Or by wanting to fool around, for that matter.)

He doesn't have to worry that tomorrow morning Dawn's going to tell Brielle and Kyla what a slut he is, and act like they really did something they didn't, or tell Brielle and Kyla that he came onto her and she turned him down because he's too ugly, or fat, or he smells bad.

He doesn't have to worry that his whole reputation (albeit in this stupid, self-contained Out of the Wild messed-up ecosystem) is ruined because he did or didn't do what a girl wanted.

He's not a girl.

Hence, he's snoring, while Dawn lies awake.

And after Dawn's reminded herself there are bigger things going on than how she didn't mess around with the cute guy, her mind pushes Warden aside and focuses on the bigger picture instead.

She's scared.

The storm is howling outside, battering the walls of the tent. She would *no shit* be dying of hypothermia if she'd slept under the tarp.

(She hopes Christian is okay, up at the summit.)

She's scared of the mountain and scared of this storm and she's scared of what Warden's proposing to do.

Abandon the counselors.

Set out into THE WILD on their own.

Escape everyone and everything that got them here to this disaster.

Dawn is scared that Warden won't be able to do what he promised.

And a part of her is scared that he will.

She sleeps eventually.

She's too tired not to. It's been a long day. It's been a long week.

It's been a long life since Cam and Wendy had her kidnapped.

Even the storm and Warden's incessant snoring can't keep her awake forever.

Eventually, Dawn drifts off.

It's a deep, dreamless sleep.

And when she wakes up, it's daylight, and Warden is gone.

6O.

WARDEN HASN'T GONE FAR.

Dawn can hear his voice outside the tent, and she can smell and hear a fire burning, and hear Brandon and Evan laughing, and Kyla saying something sharp and probably hilarious.

(She doesn't hear Lucas, and she thinks about their little tiff last night, keeps running her mind over it like you run your tongue over a sore tooth, and she thinks about what happened between her and Warden last night, too, and tries to figure out how she should feel about it all, and then she unzips the tent flap and looks out at the tarn and she forgets about Lucas and Kyla and Warden and even Amber.)

Because there's snow.

Everywhere.

Two things happen when Dawn pokes her head out of Warden's tent:

1) A big pile of snow collapses from the top of the tent onto her head and down the back of her shirt, and
2) A fluffy white snowball creams her in the face.

Dawn shrieks at the snow down her back, but the sound comes out muffled because her mouth is full of snow from the snowball, and she hears Warden laughing as she ducks back into the tent.

"Wakey-wakey, sleeping beauty," he calls, but not unkindly. "Your breakfast is getting cold."

It's at that moment Dawn realizes she's ravenously hungry and that whatever Warden and the others are cooking over the fire smells delicious.

She pulls on her jacket and her boots and steps out into winter, where the storm has abated but the snow is still falling, peaceful but steady, and everything, tents and boulders and mountain, is covered in a fresh blanket of snow.

"Holy crap," she says, looking around, dazed.

(The top of the Raven's Claw is obscured by clouds. The ridge opposite is visible, though, and it's a pristine layer of white, rendered dull and muted under low-lying gray cloud and the snow.)

It's a strange, quiet world.

"Crazy, right?" Warden says, and he hands her a mug of something hot and steaming that smells just like coffee. "You would have died under that tarp last night."

Dawn takes a sip, and it is coffee, and she wants to kiss him again or at least ask him where the hell he found it; she hasn't had coffee since she left Sacramento.

Warden winks at her. "Christian's secret stash," he says. "I figured he's not going to miss it."

The mention of Christian makes Dawn look up at the Raven's Claw again. Warden follows her gaze. "He's fine," he tells her. "Like I said, he would have been cold last night, but he had shelter up there. But if he has any sense, he'll come down to a lower altitude where it's warmer, so we need to get moving, right?"

He's smiling at her, the kind of smile that instantly makes her feel five or ten degrees warmer.

Hell, even Brandon and Evan aren't looking at her like they're secretly laughing, like Warden's been telling stories while she's asleep in his tent.

(They're too busy throwing snowballs at her.)

Dawn sips her coffee, and the coffee is good. And for a moment she forgets she was ever worried about anything.

"Where's Lucas?" she asks.

Kyla rolls her eyes. "He's fine," she says. "He's in his tent. I just brought him coffee and breakfast." She gives Dawn a look like woman to woman, like she knows Lucas is sulking and she knows why.

Dawn feels herself go red and changes the subject. "Did Alex leave already?"

It might be Dawn's imagination, or it might not be, and even if it isn't her imagination, it might mean nothing or it might mean more, but she thinks she sees a shadow cross Warden's face for a second.

"He's gone," Warden says. He gestures down the trail, across the trench and to the ridge opposite, back toward headquarters. "He left for help early this morning. So as soon as we eat breakfast, we've got to pack up and go. Put some distance in before the rescue team arrives."

Dawn shivers. She squints across the trench at the ridge on the other side, looking for any sign of Alex, like maybe footprints or the telltale yellow of his Bear Cub jacket, but she can't see anything.

"Hurry up and eat," Warden says. "I'll pack our stuff and then we'll hit the trail."

The word *eat* reminds Dawn that she's ravenous. She doesn't know where the others found bacon, but she can smell it cooking, and she wants it.

And she forgets about Alex, for the time being.

61.

THE FIRST PART of Warden's escape route is the same way they took to get up to the Raven's Claw in the first place. They have to drop down into that very deep, narrow trench that separates the tarn from the ridge on which Dawn embarrassed herself by crying about her nana to Warden.

If they were going back to Out of the Wild headquarters, they would climb out of the trench and up onto the ridge and continue south.

By Warden's reckoning, they need to follow the trench east as it swings around the base of the Raven's Claw and eventually joins the river that they'll follow northeast to the highway.

It's still early morning when they set out from the tarn and start down into the trench. Dawn's backpack feels weird on her shoulders after going the better part of a day without wearing it. Her legs, though, and her feet still remember how much hiking sucks. She's feeling her blisters within the first fifteen minutes.

Only nineteen and three-quarter miles to go.

Lucas falls in beside her. He doesn't say anything for a little while, as they navigate the steep trail. Then he glances at her. "So we're really doing this, huh?"

Dawn shrugs. "I guess so."

"You really trust Warden to get us out of here?"

"He saw the counselors' map," Dawn says. "He has a photographic memory."

"Ah," Lucas says. "Right."

"Anyway, why did you come if you don't trust him?" she asks. "You could have gone back to headquarters with Alex if you're really that worried."

Lucas hesitates.

"I just think we all need to be careful," he says.

Dawn looks over at him, and Lucas meets her eyes, and Dawn can see he's as nervous as she is. "We'll be fine," she says, though she doesn't quite believe it. "In a couple of days, we'll be back in civilization."

They stop for water when they reach the bottom of the trench and prepare to branch off from the trail back to headquarters. They've dropped maybe six hundred, seven hundred feet, back below the tree line, and it's warmer down here and darker, overgrown by trees and moss and ferns. There's less snow, just patches here and there; the trench is only about forty feet wide.

Dawn has to pee. She curses herself for not going before they left the campsite, but in her defense the whole Pack was waiting on her, and anyway, she didn't really have to go.

She has to go now, though. She tells Lucas to tell the others to wait for her a minute, and then she slips off into the trees to find somewhere private.

It seems like an embarrassing inconvenience at the time. Within minutes, it will have life-changing implications, for Dawn and for everyone else.

62.

DAWN FINDS HERSELF AT THE BASE of a cliff. She can just hear the sound of the Pack's voices in the distance, but she's far enough away that nobody will accidentally get a show if they look in her direction.

The cliff extends high above Dawn, reaching back up toward the Raven's Claw and the tarn and the trail, a sheer, uninterrupted drop. There's a pile of snow at the base of it, and a couple of fallen logs that Dawn thinks she could lean against as she pees. She pushes her way through the forest toward those fallen logs, and she's halfway to where she wants to be when she sees it.

And she wouldn't even see it if she hadn't slipped a little bit, nearly tripped over a hidden root and stumbled forward and had to catch herself on a tree branch before she faceplanted, but she was already almost on the ground anyway, and from her position more or less on her knees, she peered forward underneath the fallen log that was her objective and directly at the bottom of the cliff and the boulders and big piles of snow at the base of it.

And that's where she sees it.

She's not even sure what it is, not at first. Just a flash of color in an otherwise monochrome land, color too bright and vibrant and obnoxious to occur naturally in nature.

This color is chemical. Cooked up in a lab. Probably created out of plastic and some assortment of weird poisonous dyes. This color stands out amid the white and the black and the various shades of gray, even though it's just a scrap mostly buried in snow and obscured by rocks and trees.

This color is yellow, bright yellow.

It's the color of Alex's Bear Cub jacket.

63.

DAWN HAS NEVER SEEN a dead body before. Not in person.

Aside from that little scrap of jacket, Alex is almost completely buried in the snow. He's buried enough that Dawn can almost fool herself that it's only a jacket she's seeing, not a body.

Almost, but not quite.

Dawn picks her way cautiously up to the scrap of yellow jacket, as if it's somehow going to come to life and, I don't know, attack her or something.

"Hello?" she says, and her voice shakes and she's irrationally embarrassed about that, somewhere in the part of her brain that isn't cold and really scared and still kinda has to pee. The scrap of yellow jacket that may or may not be attached to a body does not respond.

Dawn creeps up right beside the scrap of yellow jacket that may or may not be a body, and it doesn't move, and there's too much snow to tell straight away if it's a body or not.

She nudges the snow with the toe of her boot and it doesn't

really give very much, but it certainly feels squishier than a rock.

It feels like a person who has been lying under the snow for a while.

Dawn tries to kick the snow away, but she's uncoordinated and graceless and she nearly slips and falls onto the scrap of yellow jacket that may or may not be a body, so she stops trying to kick the snow away.

She looks around the bottom of the cliff as though someone is going to show up to make this any easier.

As far as she can tell, she's alone.

She crouches down in the snow beside the scrap of yellow jacket that, let's face it, is probably attached to a body. Holds her breath. Reaches out with a fair amount of, you know, trepidation, and wipes some snow off the jacket.

There's enough give underneath the jacket that she knows it's not rocks under there. Someone or something is wearing this jacket.

Dawn brushes more snow off, and there's a zipper and a couple of pockets, which really sucks because it means she's touching the front of the jacket, which means somewhere above where she's touching, well . . .

There's going to be a face.

64.

IT TAKES SOME TIME, but she does it.

It takes a lot of breathing through her nose and trying not to be sick, and trying to tell herself that even if this *is* Alex under all of this snow, he's dead now, completely dead, and he can't do anything to her.

She wraps her hand in the sleeve of her jacket. Holds her breath again and kind of looks away. Reaches out to where she imagines the face should be, and as, lightly as she can, brushes the snow clear.

She lets out her breath.

Tries to well up her courage. *Be a damn Grizzly.*

Dawn forces herself to look at the body. At the face.

It's Alex.

At first glance, he looks normal.

Dawn tries not to do more than glance at him; she looks just long enough to see that it's Alex, and he's dead.

(His eyes are open. He's not moving. He's buried under snow. He's dead.)

This should be enough. She's done her job. She's found the body and confirmed that it is in fact a body.

That it's Alex's body.

She can go back to the others and report this with her head held high, feeling like a Grizzly Bear and not a Bear Cub, and she can tell Warden and the others and they can all as a group decide what to do next.

But some sick side of Dawn is actually curious. She can't *not* look, now that she's gone to the trouble. She glances back at Alex. Brushes a little more snow off.

And now she can see how *not normal* he really looks.

There's something wrong with his eyes, for one thing. They're open but not open, like he's blind or something. They're a weird kind of *not* color, so he doesn't look entirely like Alex anymore.

Plus, his face is messed up.

It looks like somebody kicked the shit out of him. He's got bruises and cuts and swelling everywhere. Dawn surmises this must be what happens when you plummet six hundred feet to your death.

(She's thankful, for once, that they're high in the mountains and that summer is over. No way could she handle it if there were, like, *bugs* on the body.)

Dawn lets herself look away from the body. She looks up the cliff face and it's jagged and black and sharp as far as she can see. She can easily imagine he picked up the bruises and cuts on the way down, when he fell. If anything kicked the shit out of him, it was probably nature.

But that still leaves the question:

Who in the Bear Pack *stabbed* him?

AUTHOR'S NOTE

OH YEAH. SORRY.

    Aside from the bruises and the minor cuts and scrapes that Dawn can see and infer must have come from the fall, well . . .

                                       There's a big jagged

                                             bloody

                                         wound

                                 in Alex's chest.

    It's not the kind of thing that just happens when you fall.

65.

ALEX IS LYING FACEUP. His eyes are open. He would have died seeing the sky, seeing the snow fall.

Did he know it would bury him?

Did he wonder if anyone would ever find him?

I found you, Dawn thinks. *But how did you get here?*

And who did this to you?

The counselors had a knife. And bear spray. But Christian didn't stab Alex, and neither did Amber.

That means it was someone in the Pack.

Dawn stares down at Alex and his bloody, jagged wound, and she sure as hell has her suspicions who did it, but—before she can really explore them—someone sneaks up behind her.

"What are you doing?"

A hand grabs Dawn's shoulder, rough, and Dawn screams before she can stop herself, turns around, flailing, to find Brandon standing over her, his hands up to defend himself. "Whoa," he says, stepping back. "Holy shit, Dawn. Just relax."

Slowly, Dawn stands, the sound of her scream echoing up the wall of the cliff and along the bottom of the trench. She can hear alarmed voices through the forest; the rest of the Pack, coming to investigate.

They're coming, Dawn thinks, *and now we'll get some answers.*

Brandon doesn't try to touch her again. He stands in front of her, just a little too close, watching her and not saying anything.

There's something weird about him, and Dawn realizes it's that he's not smiling his usual stupid smile, the one where it looks like he's laughing at you for some reason and you have no idea what. The one where it looks like he believes you're stupid and he's better than you and you just haven't figured it out yet.

(And maybe you never will.)

He's not smiling. He's just watching her, cold.

It's unsettling.

"What are you doing?" he asks her again.

(It's weird to see Brandon without Evan, too. Weird to think of him as a separate entity when he's usually just one half of the clown posse, or at best Warden's minion. It's weird to see Brandon thinking for himself.)

(It's scary to imagine what he might be thinking about.)

"I had to pee," Dawn says, weakly. But there's no point in pretending anymore; Brandon can see Alex's body. "Alex is dead," she says.

Brandon doesn't react. He doesn't react, and his nonreaction is scarier than anything else.

"That sucks," he says.

"Yeah," Dawn replies.

"No, I mean it sucks that you found him. That's a real fucking trip."

He looks at her for a long time. Finally, he squares his shoulders and seems to decide something.

But whatever it is, it'll have to wait. Because it's at that moment the rest of the Pack emerges from the forest.

66.

WARDEN LEADS the rest of the Pack into the clearing at the base of the cliff.

(Before anyone else in the Pack can see, and while Brandon's turned away to greet Warden, Dawn kicks snow over Alex's body.)

(She has her reasons.)

"What the hell's going on?" Warden asks Brandon and Dawn. "We're wasting time here, you guys. We need to keep moving."

"She found Alex," Brandon says before Dawn can say anything.

Dawn steps to one side, revealing what's still visible of Alex's body. "Yeah," she says, "I did."

Kyla gasps. Lucas swears. Brielle shakes her head and leans closer. Frowns as she studies the body.

"Holy shit," Warden says. He rushes across the clearing to Dawn. Takes her hands. "Dawn, I'm so sorry."

Why? Dawn thinks. *I'm not dead.*

Lucas rubs his face. Looks up the cliff wall. "I don't get it," he says. "How did he end up all the way down here?"

"He must have gotten lost," Evan says. "He left early this morning. Probably he just went the wrong way and just tumbled."

The rest of the Pack nods, and stares down at the body. It's as good an explanation as anything they're going to get.

Only Brandon doesn't react. He doesn't take his eyes away from Dawn.

(And Dawn's getting a creepy feeling, and, reader, you *know* why she's getting a creepy feeling.)

(And you know she's probably right.)

"This doesn't change anything," Warden says. "It's sad to say, and it's shitty for Alex, but we can't let this slow us down."

The Pack gathers around him, and it's clear Warden is the Leader and they're all looking at him to tell them what comes next.

"But what about Amber?" Dawn asks. "Now we know there's no rescue coming."

Warden takes her hand. "There's still a rescue," he tells her. "When we get to the highway tomorrow we'll flag someone down. We'll tell them Amber and Christian are still out here. If we hurry, we can get a helicopter to her before dark."

Dawn looks around at the rest of the group. Nobody's looking at anyone else.

Except Brandon is still watching Dawn.

Meanwhile, Lucas is still stealing glances at Alex's body,

then gazing up the side of the cliff and frowning. "But what was Alex doing on this side of the mountain?" he says. "This cliff is nowhere *near* the trail down from the tarn."

Warden shifts, impatiently.

"It doesn't matter," he says. "We're probably never going to know. What matters now is that we have to keep moving."

67.

SO THEY KEEP MOVING.

It doesn't feel good, but like Warden says, there's nothing they can do for Alex now. So they shoulder their packs. They fall in behind Warden. They follow the trench east, away from the trail.

And Dawn doesn't tell a soul about how Alex was stabbed.

She figures it's safer for everyone if nobody knows that she knows someone in the group murdered Alex. That it was probably Brandon or Evan.

She knows if she starts pointing fingers and raising a fuss, well, feelings are bound to get hurt. Lines will be drawn. The whole "getting out of the forest alive" situation will get a little more complicated.

Dawn figures there will be time when they get to the highway to sort through the question of who murdered Alex.

In the meantime, she just wants to survive.

So she keeps her mouth shut.

Doesn't tell a soul.

(Not even Lucas.)

68.

"I JUST DON'T LIKE IT," Lucas tells Dawn, as they hike.

They're still below the tree line, steadily dropping altitude. In the distance, Dawn can see the river toward which Warden is leading them.

The river that leads to the highway.

It's late afternoon now. The sky's getting darker. Sooner or later, they're going to have to make camp, but Warden keeps pushing them. Chewing up distance.

Warden's in a hurry, and the whole Pack is struggling to keep up.

"I keep thinking about Alex," Lucas says. They're a ways back from everyone else; nobody can hear them. "Like, how does it make sense that he fell off *that* cliff?"

Dawn shrugs. "Evan is probably right," she says. "He just got lost in the dark and went in the wrong direction."

"You'd have to be pretty stupid to mess up that badly," Lucas replies. "Do you really believe that?"

Dawn says nothing. Keeps hiking. Aware of Lucas's eyes on her.

"No," Lucas says. "You don't." He pauses. "You're just too scared to admit it."

(He's right.)

(Dawn's freaking terrified.)

Before she can say anything, though, someone screams from the trail up ahead.

And Lucas and Dawn glance at each other, and then they start running.

69.

KYLA SITS IN THE SNOW in the middle of the forest. She's clutching her ankle.

She's crying.

"I freaking *hate* nature," she says.

She tries to stand, and she can't. Not even with Warden's help.

("Stepped on a root or something," Warden explains to Dawn. "She twisted her ankle. I don't think it's broken.")

Broken or not, Kyla isn't walking any farther tonight.

The Pack will have to make camp.

They find a bit of a clearing to set up their tents. It's not big enough for everyone; Lucas takes one look at where Warden's setting up, and he disappears through some trees to another patch of flat ground.

Brielle sets up her tent somewhere out of sight, too.

It's nearly dark by the time they get everything unpacked and the water boiling for dinner. Dawn's tired and cold and hungry, and she knows Warden's waiting for her to move her stuff into his tent and it will be warm in there and she can rest for a while, but something's holding her back.

"What's up?" Warden asks as he watches Dawn unroll her tarp and look around for a couple of suitable trees. "You know you can crash with me again. I promise I won't try anything."

Dawn can't meet his eyes. "It's not that," she says.

"Then what?"

Dawn doesn't answer. Wonders if she should tell Warden about what she saw, what she's afraid of. Wonders what he would do if he knew Brandon or Evan was a killer.

"Dawn," Warden says. He takes hold of her shoulders and turns those green eyes on her. "You know you can talk to me, right?"

Dawn's certain that line works on most girls.

(With those eyes? *Dynamite.*)

It might work on her, too, in a different situation.

But Dawn has trust issues at this point in time. She's not sure who she trusts or what she believes. So Warden's magnet eyes don't quite captivate her; she gazes down at her feet first, and then at Warden's tent, and he's left the flap open in his haste to reassure her, and Dawn can see inside, see his pile of Polar Bear clothes and his nice camping backpack, and the nice headlamp and camp stove he must have earned while he was in the program.

And there's something else in there, too. Something bright

and shiny, and it catches the light from Dawn's headlamp and gleams back at her. And Dawn can't figure out what it is at first, and then she does and it all comes together, and suddenly she's more scared than she's ever been before in her life.

70.

IT'S THE KNIFE. Christian's knife.

That's what's in Warden's tent. The knife that Christian should still be holding on to, way up high near the top of the Raven's Claw.

The knife that is the Pack's only weapon. That probably murdered Alex.

The knife is in Warden's tent.

Alex was *stabbed* to death.

What the actual fuck?

71.

IT'S SUDDENLY VERY COLD where Dawn is standing. And no sweater, no sleeping bag, no roaring fire can change that. Dawn is suddenly very aware of how alone she is here in the clearing, even with Warden and the others nearby.

"Dawn?" Warden says again.

He shifts his position a little, turns to follow her gaze, and Dawn looks quickly away from Warden's tent and prays he doesn't realize she's seen the knife.

Her thoughts are racing.

She can't figure it out.

Did Warden kill Alex?

And if Warden has Christian's knife . . . what happened to Christian?

Dawn forces herself to meet Warden's eyes. "Thanks so much for the offer," she tells him, smiling. "It's really kind of you, but I think I'll just sleep somewhere else tonight."

Warden blinks.

Then his eyes narrow.

(For a heart-stopping moment, Dawn imagines that he can read her mind, that he knows *she* knows.)

But instead, Warden just shrugs. "Suit yourself."

———

So Dawn sleeps in Kyla's tent that night. But Dawn can't sleep.

The wind is picking up again. Dawn lies awake and listens to it blow and hears the first spatter of rain against the thin tent material.

She can't sleep because she's afraid if she sleeps that whoever killed Alex will sneak up and surprise her.

Dawn is scared.

She's scared of the night, and she's scared of what might happen in the morning.

She's scared of what the knife in Warden's tent means. She's scared it means he, not Brandon or Evan, murdered Alex.

She's scared because she's trusting Warden to get them out of here. And she's scared because he might not be who she thinks he is.

She's scared nobody will believe her if she tells them.

She's scared that even if Warden isn't a killer he'll still get them lost, that another storm will kick up and Warden's memory will fail him, or the map he remembers will be wrong, and they'll all of them die out here in the wilderness.

She's scared that Amber's still alive and they're leaving her to die.

But what scares Dawn most of all is knowing how easily

she could forget about all of it. Knowing she could just walk away.

She doesn't want to. She knows it's not right that Alex is dead. That Amber is probably dying, if she isn't dead already.

That Christian is alone on the top of the Raven's Claw.

(If he isn't dead already, too.)

Dawn knows a strong, good-hearted person would find a way to fight for the truth and for justice and whatever other words sound like solid unmovable mountains when you're snug in your bed but seem like bullshit when you're camping in a blizzard with murderers.

Dawn knows she should fight harder, for Alex and Amber and even for Christian.

But she knows in the morning there's a fair chance she'll pack up with the rest of the group and set off down the trail after Warden and not say anything and maybe never say anything.

She's tired and she's hungry and scared, and she knows there's an easy way out.

If she keeps her mouth shut, she doesn't have to be so scared.

72.

IT'S HER DAD WHO CONVINCES HER.

Now, Dawn doesn't believe in ghosts. And the ghost of her dad doesn't visit her in Kyla's tent. Not, like, in a spiritual form. But as Dawn lies awake listening to the rain fall, she's thinking about her dad anyway.

Dawn's dad was a good man. He was kind and funny and generous. He was an accountant and he worked a lot, but he always made time to hang out with his children.

Help Dawn with her homework.

Take Dawn and Bryce out for ice cream on hot summer nights.

Watch movies.

Take walks.

He was a good dad, and he loved his kids. And he was always trying to teach them about Doing the Right Thing. Doing the Right Thing was important to Dawn's dad. It was a big sticking point.

Find someone's wallet on the ground? Give it back to them.

Make a mistake? Own up to it.

"Even if it's not the easiest path," he'd tell Dawn and Bryce, "do it anyway. In the long run, you'll be rewarded."

Dawn's dad was all about Doing the Right Thing.

(Of course, in the end, it was Doing the Right Thing that got Dawn's dad killed, but never mind that for a moment.)

Dawn knows that leaving Amber and Christian to die on the mountain is not the Right Thing to Do. She knows that letting one of the Pack members get away with murdering Alex is not the Right Thing, either.

She knows, as painful as it is to admit it, that following the Pack out to the highway and bailing for Chicago to see Nana is not the Right Thing. Not when Amber's still out there and she might be alive.

Not when someone in the Pack stabbed Alex to death.

(Somewhere inside of her, Dawn knows that Cam and Wendy believed they were Doing the Right Thing by sending her to Out of the Wild. She knows that running away to live with a drug dealer was emphatically the *wrong thing* to do. She knows that she hasn't been Doing the Right Thing for a long while now, probably ever since her dad died.)

(But that doesn't mean she can't start.)

As quickly and as quietly as she can, Dawn gathers her supplies in Kyla's tent.

Warm clothes.

Camp stove.

Water pump.

(Just the basics.)

She leaves the books behind. Too heavy. She doesn't pack her sleeping bag, either, or her tarp, for the same reason.

(She's going to need to be quick.)

It will take two days to get to headquarters, she imagines. She'll be lighter and faster on her own than with the rest of the group, but the storm's coming back, and that's going to be a big problem.

The weather will slow her down, make it hard to navigate. It's going to be a difficult hike. But what choice does she have? Amber's depending on her. And Alex deserves justice.

Going for help is the Right Thing to Do.

When Dawn has her bag packed, she slowly, gingerly, leans over and unzips the tent flap. Pulls her jacket tight around her and laces up her hiking boots and slips out into the storm.

(Behind her, Kyla stirs, but she doesn't wake up.)

It's nearly pitch dark and the rain is starting to spatter.

The wind is blowing and the air is raw.

Any normal person would just crawl back in their sleeping bag and zip the tent closed, and Dawn's really tempted to do just that. But she keeps thinking about her dad, and what he would want her to do.

And she knows it isn't even a question.

Dawn raids the Pack's stash of food. Lowers the bag down from the tree where it's hanging and turns on her headlamp and combs through it.

Thing is, there isn't much food left. Dawn manages to salvage a couple of canteens and a pot. Emergency matches. Some energy bars and some trail mix, a pack of rehydration gummy candies. Two backpacker meals—Santa Fe Chicken and Bombay Delight—and three packages of instant oatmeal. She leaves the lentils.

It's not much food for a solid two-day hike. Dawn knows she'll be starving by the time she gets to headquarters, but so be it. Those Out of the Wild office nerds can cook her a freaking buffet when she gets there.

Dawn zips up her backpack. Buckles it closed. Lifts it onto her shoulders and fastens the straps. It's lighter without her tarp and the books and her sleeping bag, so that's a plus. All that remains is to take the first step, and the next.

All that remains is to Do the Right Thing.

But of course it's never that easy.

73.

DAWN'S CREEPING PAST the other tents when she sees him. Warden, sitting at the remains of last night's fire, now just smoldering, flickering charcoal and ash.

Smoke, and cold rain.

Warden's sitting on a log with his hoodie pulled up. At first, he looks like a statue, or any one of the boys, but then a log pops and blows sparks in the air, and Dawn can see that it's Warden.

And she can see that he's watching her.

"What are you doing?" Warden asks. He stares at her, not moving, his face half engulfed in shadow and his voice chillingly calm. Beside him on the log sits Christian's knife and Amber's bear spray. Dawn tries not to focus on the knife, tries to meet Warden's eyes.

She doesn't say anything, and Warden picks up the knife. He stands and walks toward her. "Dawn?" he says. "I asked you a question."

Dawn is terrified.

Naturally.

She feels her whole body start to shake involuntarily and she prays that Warden can't tell. His face dissolves into shadow as he moves away from the fire, and he's just a silhouette and the silhouette is holding a knife.

Dawn swallows and tries not to look scared. "Where did you get that knife?" she asks.

Warden glances down at the blade in his hand. "This thing?" he says. He studies it, absentmindedly. Turns the blade over in his hand, watching how it catches the light. "It's Christian's knife."

"I know that," Dawn says. "So how did you . . . ?"

Warden looks up sharply. Dawn can't see his eyes, but she can tell they're boring into her, reading her soul. "I took it from him," he says. "On the top of the Claw."

It's at that moment Dawn knows that Christian is dead.

Because she knows Christian, and Christian wouldn't give up his knife. Not to a Pack member and especially not to Warden. She knows if Warden took the knife from Christian, it wasn't with Christian's permission. That means they must have fought for it. Warden walked away with the knife.

Dawn knows that means Christian didn't walk away, period.

Warden must see the moment of realization in Dawn's eyes.

"*Fuck* Christian," he says, and Dawn steps back, surprised by the ferocity in his voice. "He was a prison guard, just like Amber. Just like the rest of them. He wasn't a good person, and he deserved what he got."

Dawn doesn't say anything. She might be on board with this line of thinking. The counselor was a creep, after all. He'd been torturing Kyla for months. He wasn't a good person, and if someone had to die, then maybe it's best it was Christian.

But Christian's not the only one who's dead.

"What about Alex?" Dawn asks. "What did he do wrong?"

It's impossible to see Warden's face to tell how he reacts. But what Dawn can tell, he doesn't move. He doesn't speak for a long period of time.

And then he laughs. "I guess you saw more of Alex than I thought," he says. "You weren't supposed to figure it out."

Dawn says nothing. Her heart is pounding.

"It would have looked like an accident," Warden says. "By the time anyone found him the animals would have had their way with his body. No one would ever know how he died."

Dawn tries to speak but her mouth is too dry. She wets her lips. "Why?"

Warden shrugs. "He was a liability. He would have raised the alarm at headquarters, and that would have cost us time."

Warden says, "He knew where we were going."

He says, "He chose to abandon the rest of the Pack."

And then he shrugs again.

"Also," he says, "I just didn't like how he tried to play hero."

74.

"SO YOU SEE WHY we can't let you leave," Warden says.

Dawn stares at him.

"You're a part of the team, Dawn," he tells her. "We have to all stick together. I can't let you go back to headquarters, not now that you know."

Warden takes a step forward, and Dawn sees how the firelight glints off the knife. "You're either with us, or against us," Warden tells her. "Whose side are you on, Dawn? The prisoners, or the guards?"

"Think carefully," Warden says. "There's only one Correct Answer."

It goes without saying this is not exactly the situation Dawn's dad had in mind when he preached to her about Doing the Right Thing.

Or maybe it is.

Dawn stares at the shadow that is Warden and the glinting knife. And she knows she's seeing the true Warden now, and whoever she was falling for before wasn't him. And she knows she was foolish to even follow him this far.

Warden watches her. He shifts the knife in his hand.

"Silence," he says, "will be considered an Incorrect Answer."

Dawn knows there's no way out of this mess. She knows that in a moment Warden's either going to:

a) Do something awful, or
b) Wake up Brandon and Evan, and they'll do the awful thing for him.

She can't outrun Warden, not for long. But if she stays here, she's probably dead anyway. No way Warden lets her live, not now that she knows he killed Alex. Not now that he knows she wants to escape.

She holds her head high and stares at the shadows that obscure Warden's face. "I'm leaving," she tells him. "That's my answer."

It sounds brave and badass, and for an instant, it makes Dawn feel pretty good. But then Warden lunges for her and grabs her and wrenches her forward, and he's too strong for Dawn by a mile and he pulls her off-balance and staggering toward the fire, and Warden keeps dragging her until she's falling forward, until she's on her knees in the mud.

And then she looks up, and Warden's raising the knife.

Dawn opens her mouth to scream. It's all she has left and

she knows it isn't much. But Warden's raising the knife and the fire's catching his eyes and she can see how he looks at her and there's no *Warden* there—at least, not the guy she thought she knew.

"I told you," Warden says, "you're not leaving."

Dawn opens her mouth to scream. Hoping that somehow if she screams, it will stop him. It will bring the others to help her.

It will save her life.

She opens her mouth to scream, but before she can get the words out . . .

Warden screams instead.

75.

THERE'S AN EXPLOSION.

(Not, like, a *boom* but a tremendous *hissss.*)

And then Warden's screaming and clutching at his eyes. He's slashing around—blind—with Christian's big knife. And Lucas is standing behind him with Amber's can of bear spray.

(The spray is so potent that Dawn's eyes start to water and she's suddenly finding it hard to breathe.)

Lucas lifts her to her feet. Pulls her away from the fire and where Warden is crouched on the ground now, gagging. Lucas pulls Dawn away from the tents. Toward the trail that leads back to the Raven's Claw.

"Come on," he tells her. "Before everyone else wakes up."

There's nothing to do but start running.

By the light of their headlamps, following the sketchy trail through the mud and the snow that their feet trampled into existence that afternoon. Up toward the barrier trench and the Raven's Claw and the trail toward help.

There's nothing to do but start running, and they do.

Run, and hope nobody follows.

Behind them, the forest is silent. The trail is steep and slippery and Dawn almost bails a couple of times, and when she stops to catch her balance and regain her breath she listens, and she can't hear Warden behind them or anyone else, just the rain and Lucas beside her, trying to catch his own breath.

There's no time to be scared anymore. They pause for a second and then they run again, certain that they're dead if they're caught. They run and gain altitude and the rain turns to snow and it soaks through Dawn's pants and her boots and she's sweating through her undershirt, and her hands and her knees are covered in mud and wet from slipping and crawling and trying to pull herself up.

Around them, the night grows imperceptibly lighter. Morning is coming, but that doesn't matter.

All that matters is getting away.

76.

AFTER A TIME, THEY REACH the barrier trench, sweaty and out of breath and exhausted. It's darker in the trench but steadily getting lighter, night turning inexorably to day.

Briefly, they stop to sip water out of one of Dawn's canteens, and Dawn transfers as much food as she can into Lucas's pockets.

There's blood on his jacket. A tear in the lining. "Warden's knife," Lucas tells her. He pulls the jacket tighter; he won't let her see. "It's just a scratch," he says. "I'll be fine."

Dawn studies his face. He stares back at her, earnest, and Dawn knows he's probably lying, that he's hurt worse than he's ready to admit. But there's no point in pushing him right now.

(She didn't steal the first-aid kit from the Pack.)

"What were you even doing out there, anyway?" she asks Lucas. "Shouldn't you have been, like, asleep?"

"I had to pee," he says, sheepishly. "I saw you and Warden in the light of the fire. I thought—" He looks away. "I just had to know for sure that you like him."

Dawn makes a face. "I don't like him," she says. "He's a

freaking *murderer*, Lucas." She explains to him what she knows about Warden. About Christian and Alex.

"You didn't tell me?" Lucas says. "You knew Alex was murdered and you didn't want to tell me?"

"I just thought it was safer if no one knew that I knew," Dawn tells him. "I didn't want to tip off the killer."

Lucas doesn't say anything, and Dawn can tell he's hurt. They stand there in silence and drink a little more water.

"Anyway, thanks," Dawn says. "For saving my life."

The trail up the south side of the trench is steeper than the trail up to the Raven's Claw tarn. Dawn and Lucas pull themselves skyward using tree roots as handholds, the weight on Dawn's back threatening to pull her down again to the bottom, send her falling to her death.

Dawn's legs are burning. Her knees hurt and her hands are numb. But she can't afford to stand around feeling sorry for herself.

(Lucas was, after all, *stabbed*. And he seems to be doing okay.)

Gradually, Dawn and Lucas climb out of the trees again, and back into the falling snow and the wind. It's light enough now that they don't need flashlights, and if they look back across the barrier trench, Dawn and Lucas can see the shadowy visage of the Raven's Claw looming over them.

Ahead of them is more bare rock, a trail marked by cairns across the alpine. Dawn knows they'll follow this ridge for a few hours before they descend again to the lakes where they camped, and then after that, they'll climb up to another ridge, a longer ridge, and after that they'll drop back into the forest and follow the trail toward headquarters.

Dawn remembers how long it took to hike this far from headquarters. How tired she was.

It seems like a LONG WAY AWAY.

She was walking right here when she and Warden traded Origin Stories, Dawn remembers. Following this ridge but in the opposite direction, the Raven's Claw looming ahead of them and nothing but blue sky around it, no hint to the drama and awfulness that waited for them on the mountain.

She walks beside Lucas away from the Raven's Claw, and Lucas doesn't say anything, just keeps hiking, one foot in front of the other, and Dawn thinks about Warden and how she might have actually fallen for him, and she feels stupid and naive and kind of hates herself for it.

But also, she kind of misses that moment, too.

If that makes any sense.

Lucas walks quietly beside her, solid and dependable and never missing a step, a golden retriever with a job to do. He doesn't look scared anymore.

They hike in silence, steadily climbing through fresh snow, marking their progress by the little rock-pile cairns that sit half buried on top of bare rock. Above them, the weather is calming, the snow easing off, and they can start to see a couple of cairns ahead, start to see the mountains on either side of the ridge and the valleys in between them, the dark, inky-black lakes where they're headed.

Lucas says nothing, and Dawn says nothing, and they keep

moving forward, one foot in front of the other. And for a while it's like they're completely alone, like they're the only people left alive in the world.

It's the howling that chases that train of thought from Dawn's station.

77.

IT'S NOT WOLVES THAT ARE HOWLING. That might almost be better. It's not any wild animal making those noises,
strange and unnerving and otherworldly, echoing up from the
bottom of the trench.

(If you've ever heard a wolf howl, it sounds, well, *romantic*.
Lonely and plaintive and wild. These howls are not romantic;
there's a cruelty to them that's hard to explain. Like a gleeful,
chilling, mocking quality that immediately scares the shit out
of Dawn.)

Lucas glances back, over his shoulder. His eyes go wide.
Then, suddenly, he pulls Dawn to the ground, nearly toppling
her over onto her backpack.

"What the hell?"

They wind up behind a boulder. Lucas grips the shoulder
strap of Dawn's backpack, holding her in place, as they peer
over the top of the boulder toward the Raven's Claw.

The storm has dissipated entirely now. The Claw stands tall
and proud in all of its evil, jagged glory. It's covered in fresh
snow, but the sheer rock faces are black. Looking up at the

mountain, Dawn can't believe they were ever near the summit. She can't believe Amber fell down one of those black faces of rock and lived, however briefly.

She can see the tarn now, too. The tarn and the boulder fields are probably two or three miles away over vast, open air, but Dawn can see them, and the tarn is a black speck like a pimple against the white of the mountain.

But the howls steal her focus back before too long.

(Picture those smug, self-righteous smirks that Brandon and Evan are always wearing. Now imagine those smirks as a noise, except totally unhinged, and that's what the howls sound like.)

The howling is coming from the barrier trench, and Dawn knows that means only one thing: Warden's told the others that Dawn and Lucas have turned back. And Brandon and Evan are coming to find them.

AUTHOR'S NOTE

THERE'S A FINE LITERARY TRADITION *of people getting stuck in the middle of nowhere and their whole fabric of society breaking down.*

Maybe you had to read Lord of the Flies *in class. Or, like,* Heart of Darkness.

If you did, then you kind of know what to expect here.

People find themselves in the wilderness and it doesn't take long before the rules don't apply anymore.

All of the unwritten, unspoken tenets of civilized life we take for granted?

They break down in the wilderness.

All those laws you think protect you?

They don't matter when there's no one around to enforce them.

Some people, in the wilderness, they let themselves go. They give in to the inhuman side of their brains. They build their own societies, with their own rules.

They howl at the fucking moon.

78.

DAWN AND LUCAS CAN'T SEE IT, but back at the camp, the thin fabric of society has begun to tear to shreds. They didn't see how Brandon and Evan discovered Warden by the remains of the campfire, how he coughed and choked and couldn't breathe, and then when he finally could, he told them what Dawn and Lucas had done.

They couldn't see how Brandon and Evan set out after Dawn and Lucas, the gleam in their eyes as they thought about what came next.

They can't see how killing Dawn and Lucas isn't a necessity for Brandon and Evan, a task that needs to be done, however distasteful, to ensure Pack survival.

No.

The Pack has killed twice. Alex and Christian are dead, and their deaths broke down a barrier. The rules don't matter anymore.

What Dawn and Lucas can't see, but can surely remember, is how Brandon and Evan have been outsiders from day one, lurking on the margins and not engaging with any of the Out of the Wild teachings.

Neither of them was going to be saved by this program, not while the other was around. They endured what they had to, sure. They did as little as they could while still rising through the ranks, but they weren't going to walk out of these woods any different from how they'd walked in.

And Warden recognized that, and he used it. And he's using it still.

This is the moment Brandon and Evan have been waiting for. The chains are broken. There aren't any adults anymore, and there *is* an excuse.

Warden's focused on survival, self-preservation.

Brandon and Evan want to sow chaos; it just so happens that Warden's interests align right now with the sowing of chaos.

Dawn and Lucas can't be allowed to make it to safety. To tell what they saw, what Warden has done. Not if Warden wants to survive.

So Brandon and Evan.

So chaos.

So the boys howl like animals, because the chains have come off.

79.

EVERYTHING SEEMS TO MOVE SLOWER when you're being chased. Your feet scramble through the snow trying to find traction. You slip and almost fall. The cairns you're relying on to guide you suddenly seem to shrink and turn invisible. The trail disappears.

Behind you, the howling only seems to get closer.

Dawn runs, or tries to, and feels a hopelessness pervade her, as she's slipping and falling on the icy rock and snow, knowing Brandon and Evan are coming, knowing they won't stop until they catch up.

And then?

Dawn doesn't want to think about that. It will be violence; that's all she knows. It will be violent and desperate and she'll probably die.

Dawn doesn't want to think about that right now. She shoulders her pack and quickens her stride. Digs into the snow and ignores the ache in her muscles and the fatigue behind her eyes.

From the howling behind her, she can tell that Brandon and

Evan are near the top of the trench. Ahead of her and Lucas, the ridge climbs, and Dawn knows they'll have to turn off it soon and descend down to the lake where they camped.

There is nothing to do but to get there.

One foot in front of the other.

—

They ditch the pack at the far end of the ridge. They have to. There's no choice.

"We'll be faster if we're lighter," Lucas tells her, drinking from the canteen and catching his breath. "We have to assume that the others aren't wearing full gear. They'll gain on us if we don't shed some weight."

(Lucas keeps his arm across the tear in the front of his jacket, so Dawn can't see. She *can* see how he winces every time he moves. How he's maybe a little bit paler than normal.)

(But every time Lucas catches her looking, he turns away.)

They ditch the pot and every spare piece of clothing. The stove and the pump, everything that's weighing them down.

"We can make HQ by tomorrow morning if we push through the night," Lucas says. "We can't slow down to cook food anyway."

They fill their pockets with energy bars and trail mix and refill the canteens from a meltwater stream. Dawn studies the pile of stuff they're leaving in the snow, and none of it looks extraneous.

What if we get lost?

What if the snow starts again?

What if we don't make it back by morning?

But Lucas is right. They can't afford to slow down. They ditch both backpacker meals with the rest of the extra stuff. Dawn sheds her backpack, and they make for the tree line.

AUTHOR'S NOTE

IF YOU'RE GUESSING that Dawn and Lucas's ridding them-
selves of necessary supplies will have consequences?

You're right.

80.

IT'S FASTER WITHOUT THAT WEIGHT.

Dawn leaves her gear behind and she and Lucas follow the cairns off the ridge along a trail through a boulder field curving down to their left. They're dropping altitude again, and in the distance, Dawn can see the first of the lakes they'll have to pass before they climb to the second and final ridge. Beyond that second ridge, headquarters is maybe a half a day's hike, but just to get up on that ridge is another four hours' hike and maybe two thousand feet of elevation changes.

They're nowhere near safety.

Dawn is exhausted. She hasn't slept well since Amber fell. Even before that, she was half-dead from fatigue from all the hiking. That's the point of the Out of the Wild program, after all: grind down the bad kids until they're too tired to talk back. Until they're so broken they'll agree to do anything just to get the chance to sleep in an actual bed again.

Right now, a bed is a foreign concept. Same for a shower, or an actual meal.

But there's no point in dwelling on it. Right now, it's move or die. Dawn and Lucas descend from the first ridge toward the lakes in the distance. Beyond the second lake, Dawn can see the second ridge rising high into the sky again. Her legs ache at the thought of climbing back up to altitude. Her brain's weary and her thoughts are getting fuzzy.

But there's no point in complaining.

Dawn gobbles down a handful of trail mix and hurries to keep pace with Lucas. They keep hiking.

81.

IT'S ALMOST SCARIER when you can't hear the howling.

Dawn and Lucas descend back into forest and emerge at the end of the first of the lakes. It's long and narrow and ringed by avalanche paths: big, gigantic boulders that were a bitch to cross the first time and will be even worse in the snow.

Behind them, Brandon and Evan have stopped yelling, or maybe it's just that their voices are muffled on the other side of the ridge. Either way, it's eerily quiet down here by the lake. Dawn and Lucas could be the only people left alive in the world.

It's also beautiful here, if you can find a minute or two to stop and appreciate the surroundings. The lake is an emerald-colored jewel and the snow surrounding it is pristine, blanketing the mountainsides and the forest in unblemished white. There are no cell phones allowed in Out of the Wild, but if there were, Dawn would be an Instagram legend.

But, of course, she has other things to worry about.

She and Lucas skirt the side of the first lake, following a narrow trail between pine trees, and clamber across the avalanche fields, careful not to fall into the deep holes between the rocks. They stop to refill the canteen and drink greedily, and the water is frigid and refreshing and invigorating.

It does nothing to calm Dawn's nerves. The boys behind them have stopped howling and they could be anywhere. Dawn keeps glancing behind her, sure that Brandon and Evan are going to appear on the trail in the distance, running like killer zombies with only one thing on their minds.

She starts to think that maybe the boys have already made it *past* them, that they're waiting on the trail somewhere up ahead, planning an ambush. She tries to walk quietly, not make any noise. Strains to listen through the silence for any sound that will give away Brandon and Evan's position.

She hears nothing. Her whole body is tense, and her mind, too, like a soldier waiting for the next bomb to hit.

The boys are out there; Dawn knows it. She doesn't know where, and that's the part that really sucks. She starts to think maybe it would be better if she *could* hear them howling, just so she wouldn't feel so damn paranoid.

Then the howling starts up again, and Dawn immediately wants nothing more than to make the noise stop.

82.

SHE AND LUCAS ARE AT THE END of the first lake when they hear the howling behind them again. There's a little rise of land that separates the two lakes, and they're about at the summit of it when the noise tumbles down from high atop the ridge, blows across the lake, and assaults them with that eerie, inhuman, *predatory* laughter.

Lucas stops and turns back. Squints up at the ridgeline.

"They found our stuff," he says. "They're coming down off the ridge."

Dawn follows his gaze, but she can't see anything but snow up there. Regardless, if Lucas is right it means the boys are less than two hours' hike behind them. It means there's no time to stop and consider which Instagram filter would look best with this lake.

"Come on," Lucas says, turning to follow the trail over the rise and down toward the second lake. Dawn studies the ridgeline a moment longer. Feels her fear start to grow into panic as she thinks about what's up there.

Who's up there.

She pushes the panic down as best as she can. Turns to follow Lucas again.

The next few hours are a slog, exhausting and terrifying in equal measure. Dawn and Lucas find their way down to the second lake, the lake which they camped by on the second night of the trip. They troop past the campsite, empty and abandoned now, and Dawn sees the place where she set up her tarp, where she and Lucas argued over whether the mountain they were going to climb should be called Fart Mountain or the Raven's Claw.

Dawn sees the place where Lucas marched off to find firewood, after he'd informed her that Warden and Amber were hooking up.

And she sees the place where she lay under her tarp all night, thinking about how Warden had probably saved her life, and hoping what Lucas said wasn't true, that Warden wasn't sleeping with Amber after all.

Hoping that Warden might want to hook up with her.

She hurries past the campsite and doesn't look back.

The second lake is smaller than the first, with fewer avalanche paths to cross. They make it to the other side in decent time and find where the lake drains into a little river that they have to follow farther down, another half mile or so, before they reach the steep little valley that leads up to the second ridge.

They stop at the river and each eat a hydration candy.

"We have to start rationing," Lucas says. He says it like Dawn's been pigging out on their meager supplies, like it was *her* idea to throw the backpacker meals away.

(Like *he* actually brought any food on this misadventure.)

"We have a long way to go yet," Lucas says.

The valley up to the second ridge is steeper than Dawn remembers. And the trail is much slipperier now that it's covered in snow.

They don't have their packs, so they're lighter and can move around more easily, but still. It's a long, grueling climb, and once or twice Dawn nearly loses her footing and slides down the hillside, almost erasing an hour of work.

She catches herself just in time.

She pulls her way up the mountain until she's sweating through her undershirt and her clothes and her hands and her face are covered in mud. Until she can barely feel her fingers, which are bloody and raw and cold.

Until she emerges at the top of the valley trail into the alpine again, and the second ridge is just ahead of her and Lucas is behind her, still climbing, panting and sweating and trying to keep up, clutching at the tear in his jacket, at the wound he still won't show her underneath.

He's hurting, Dawn can tell. Hurting bad.

Maybe you should find somewhere to hide, Dawn wants to tell him. But she doesn't.

She's afraid if he lies down to rest he might not stand up again.

83.

THE BAD NEWS IS THAT IT'S afternoon at this point. From what Dawn can remember, it'll take the better part of a day to traverse the second ridge. That means they'll be doing at least some of it in darkness.

The other bad news is that the weather's turning again. As Dawn was climbing up the narrow valley, she noticed the first drops of more rain coming down through the trees. Here, in the alpine again, it's not rain but snow. Not heavy stuff, but a little bit.

And visibility is fading. Clouds are rolling in, low and dense, bringing with them wind and a penetrating moisture. Dawn stops to catch her breath and drink from the canteen and she's shivering almost instantly.

Up here, in the alpine, there are no trees for protection. Nowhere to hide from the wind or the snow. "We need to get across that ridge," she tells Lucas. "Quickly. Before the weather gets any worse."

Lucas is on board with the idea. He's lagging behind, and

visibly struggling. But he must know they could very well die of exposure if they slow down now.

So they keep climbing, up through boulders and along rocky cliffs, using lichen and shrubs and outcrops for handholds, pulling themselves higher as the clouds descend around them.

There isn't a trail up here; it's cairns again. The first few are easy to spot.

But then the cairns disappear.

"I don't get it," Lucas says, scratching his head and searching through the fog for the next pile of rocks. "I don't remember this being so hard."

They know if they follow the spine of the ridge, they probably won't get lost. So they do that. Here and there is a rock pile after all, that seems to be pointing them in the right direction.

But there were more cairns, Dawn remembers. Every fifty feet or so, clearly visible. Even with the fog, they should be able to see at least two cairns at all times, one ahead and one behind. Now, they're lucky if they can see just one.

"Are we going the right way?" Dawn asks.

"I'm pretty sure," Lucas replies, but he looks as confused as Dawn feels. "I remember that traverse right there. I remember there used to be a big old pile of rocks beside it."

It's a part of the ridge where it rises in a hump and the trail swings around the east side of it, and Dawn remembers it, too.

She thinks she remembers it was the spot where she nearly

died, where Warden saved her life. And when she thinks back, she can see the rock pile that Lucas remembers. In her mind, at least.

It's not there anymore.

———

They make the traverse anyway. Skirt around the hump and rejoin the spine of the ridge and keep going, and here and there is a sketchy trail through the alpine grass, and every now and then a rock pile.

By now the clouds have settled in so thick that it's impossible to tell which way you're walking; if Dawn and Lucas were to somehow get turned around, they could be walking back toward Brandon and Evan without ever realizing what had happened.

This is stressful. It is stressful even without knowing there are two maniacs nearby who want to kill you.

It's stressful because hypothermia is a thing and Dawn threw away most of her spare clothing, and if they get stuck on this ridgeline they could easily die.

It's stressful because it slows everything down.

Dawn and Lucas aren't running anymore, or even walking quickly. They're wandering, squinting through the fog for the next indication of where the trail goes, the ridge rising up in impassible cliff faces and sheer drops without warning, forcing them to retreat and try other directions.

Every second they waste is a second Brandon and Evan can gain on them.

But there's no other hope. There's only one way across this ridge, and if they deviate from it, Dawn knows they'll be horribly lost. They have to take the time to find the right trail, no matter how long it takes.

No matter how much it lets Brandon and Evan gain on them.

Dawn tries to focus on helping Lucas find the trail. They're standing at the top of where the ridgeline drops off, and far below she can see a path leading into the fog.

Just have to get down there, she thinks. *Then we're fine.*

But the cliff is too steep to just walk down, and Dawn knows there must be a marker somewhere to guide them. She walks along the lip of the cliff until she finds an easier descent, a notch in the side of the ridge that looks like a trail.

"Found it," she calls to Lucas, who at this point is just a ghost in the fog. She stands there and waits for him to find her.

She surveys the ground as she does.

And then she makes a terrible discovery.

84.

I DON'T KNOW IF YOU REMEMBER this part.

On the outbound hike? Before Dawn nearly fell and Warden caught her and saved her life and gave her that big lecture about making sure her pack was on the right way?

Before Dawn noticed that Warden had the greenest eyes she'd ever seen?

Before all that, but just barely, Dawn maybe noticed how Warden was lagging behind the rest of the group, when usually he walked at the front.

You know, like a leader.

But that day, when they traversed the ridge going north toward the Raven's Claw, Warden lingered near the back, and for the briefest of moments, Dawn wondered why. But then she got distracted.

She forgot about it.

What did it matter, anyway?

Well, here's why it matters: Warden was destroying those rock cairns. He was kicking those piles of rock over. Rendering them useless, just more random scree on the top of the ridge.

And I'm sure if you asked Warden why he was doing it, he'd just shrug and fix his green eyes on you and grin mischievously and tell you he was sowing the seeds of chaos. Wreaking havoc.

Causing mayhem.

There's no rational point to doing what he did, except that maybe he wanted to mess with Christian and Amber, get the group a little lost on the way back from the mountain, screw everything up and sit and laugh at the consequences.

Warden didn't know that Christian and Alex would die, obviously. He didn't know it would be Dawn and Lucas, specifically, whom he'd be screwing over.

He didn't realize that messing up the rock piles would within a few days confer on Brandon and Evan a significant strategic advantage in a particularly high-stakes race back to headquarters.

No.

But I bet if you'd told him, he would have been pretty damn pleased with himself.

85.

DAWN STARES DOWN AT THE PILE of rocks at the top of the path up the spine of the ridge. She recognizes the rocks, as weird as that sounds. She can see how this pile was once something more.

A cairn.

A guidepost.

An essential marker on their way to safety.

And now it's just rocks.

Dawn and Lucas struggle down the face of the ridge and rejoin the path at the bottom. Mercifully, the path winds through some low alpine lichen for a while, and it's easy to follow and kind of protected, so it's not as cold down here for a few minutes.

And Dawn starts to think about how Brandon and Evan won't have the cairns to guide them, either. So they'll have to slow down a little bit, assuming they aren't actual bloodhounds who can just follow Dawn's and Lucas's scent.

Even Warden, who has his photographic memory, is bound

to be slowed down by this weather. So it's not like the missing cairns give the bad guys a *huge* advantage.

Not really.

Except that all it takes for Brandon and Evan (and Warden) to win is if Dawn and Lucas can't make it to headquarters.

And right now, it's starting to get dark.

It's cold.

And it's wet on the ridge.

And Lucas is starting to stumble when he walks.

No matter how Dawn and Lucas die, if they die, Warden wins.

And no cairns means the odds of dying up here increase exponentially.

86.

NIGHT'S STARTING TO SET IN. It doesn't feel to Dawn like a full day should have passed already, but it has, and they're still on the ridge and still probably another day's hike from headquarters.

Her feet ache so bad she would gladly cut them off. The blisters on the soles of her feet have blisters. Her knees are in pain from the constant up and down on the rocks, and her thighs burn.

She's hungry. Starving. They've stopped a couple of times for handfuls of trail mix and rehydration candies, but it's not nearly enough, and as Dawn walks she thinks about food and it's torture.

She thinks about pizza and cheeseburgers and onion rings and Cherry Coke. About butter chicken and pad thai and sushi. A whole Italian feast: lasagna and spaghetti and fettuccine and chicken Parm. About hot bowls of ramen and pho and shepherd's pie and pork chops and steak.

She thinks about restaurants. All of her favorites and how if she ever gets out of here she's going to visit each and every one of them, one after the other.

McDonald's.

In-N-Out.

The Cheesecake Factory.

Olive Garden.

P.F. Chang's.

That little Indian joint down the street from her house that Cam and Wendy order takeout from.

Dawn is going to eat ALL of the things. And when she's done, she's going to march into a Dairy Queen and order a delicious Blizzard, a real Blizzard, and eat it and think about this stupid mountain and all the snow, and just be warm and enjoy her ice cream.

This is what Dawn thinks about, fantasizes about, the images she can't chase from her head as she staggers across frozen rock and snow and feels her stomach gnawing at itself and how her whole body is getting weaker and weaker.

She needs to stop and rest and slow down and sleep and eat and change out of her wet clothes and just be warm and calm and not moving and not afraid for a while.

But none of this is a possibility.

There is only more hiking.

It's getting dark outside, and Dawn's hungry.

But there's nothing on the ridge that can help her.

87.

IT'S A FEW HOURS AFTER DARK when Dawn starts to suspect they're lost.

This is never a good feeling to have and it's especially bad when you're halfway to freezing to death atop a cloud-laden mountain.

She and Lucas are navigating by flashlight and that's not a good feeling either, even with the cloud cover, because what if the clouds suddenly shift, just a little, and Brandon and Evan walk across the ridge and see the beams of light and know where they are. But Dawn keeps looking back and she doesn't see beams behind her, so maybe she's dumb to be worried about that. The *being lost* thing, though, is a serious concern.

There doesn't even seem to be a trail anymore. It's like Lucas is just following the rocks and staying on top of the ridge and hoping it'll lead them to where they're trying to go.

Which is not the worst idea in the world, given the geography and how the trail tended to follow the ridgeline. But still, Dawn can't shake the feeling that something's gone wrong, somewhere.

"Hold up," she tells Lucas. She shines her headlamp around and sees only snow and rock and Lucas, and Lucas looks tired and somehow much thinner than even this morning, as though every step he takes is leeching strength in the form of body mass.

(And he still won't let her see where Warden's knife cut him.)

"Are you sure we're headed the right way?" Dawn asks.

Lucas shines his flashlight around. "Yep," he says, after a beat. "I think so."

"I don't see a trail," Dawn tells him. "You don't think, like, we might have gotten mixed up somewhere?"

Lucas shines his flashlight at a piece of windswept rock. "There's the trail right there," he tells her.

Dawn follows his gaze. She doesn't see a trail.

"We're wasting time," Lucas says, in the way that boys sometimes do when they're sure of themselves and sick of having to explain. "Come on, Dawn. We don't want those guys catching up."

The thing is, boys use that tone that Lucas is using when they're sure about something, and when they kind of want you to know that you're NOT HELPING by asking questions.

But just because someone's sure doesn't mean that they're, you know, *right*.

(Boys especially.)

And it can be hard to differentiate between when someone actually knows what they're talking about and when they just *think* they know.

Cases like this, for instance.

But Dawn, in this instance, really has no idea if they're lost or not. And Lucas sounds pretty damn sure.

So, really, what's her choice?

Stand and argue?

Or trust Lucas?

Dawn decides that she has to trust Lucas, even though she has her doubts. "Okay," she says, shrugging. "If you're sure."

"I'm sure," Lucas says.

He starts forward again, and Dawn follows.

In hindsight, she'd have been better off standing her ground.

88.

A COUPLE OF HOURS LATER, it's clear that they *are* lost.

And by clear, I mean that the ridge they're standing on has come to its logical conclusion, and its logical conclusion is a sheer drop into pitch black with no conceivable way of descending it.

"It's too dark to tell," Lucas tells Dawn as they stand at the precipice. "The trail could be down there, like, lost in the fog. Like, just beyond our flashlight beams, or whatever."

Dawn looks around the barren ridge and picks up a piece of rock about the size of a grapefruit. She throws it over the edge of the cliff, and she and Lucas both listen to hear it hit something. They listen for a long time.

They listen for so long that Dawn starts to believe maybe the rock already landed and they just didn't hear it.

But then the sound wafts up, faint and far away, of a rock striking more rock and clattering away into nothing. The rock might as well have landed on the moon, for how far it traveled.

It's a million miles down.

Dawn and Lucas, they're standing at the edge of an abyss.

And there was no abyss on the agenda for the outbound leg of the hike.

They've dead-ended, somehow.

And that's horrible news.

By this point, Dawn is shivering. Uncontrollably. Her teeth are chattering like you only see in cartoons. Her fingers and her toes and her nose are all numb.

She can hardly think straight. But with about the last of her brainpower, she remembers how the ridge they were hiking to get to the Raven's Claw a few days ago joined with another ridge, somewhere along the way. Both ridges combined in, like, an upside-down Y, so she'd barely noticed them coming together.

But where the ridges came together on the outbound leg, they would have to branch apart on the return trip. And now Dawn realizes how easy it would have been for her and Lucas to take the wrong leg of the Y. The stub end. Especially in the dark, and with no cairns to guide them.

It's impossible to say how far they've come along this incorrect ridgeline, only that it's clear they'll have to go back.

But Brandon and Evan are back there.

And it's cold. Very cold.

Suddenly, Dawn wants nothing more than to just lie down and sleep, but however beaten down she's feeling right now? Lucas is worse.

Lucas is *pale*. His lips have a blue tinge to them and he's shivering even though he's trying not to show it. He's clutching his jacket at the spot where Warden's knife stabbed him, and his movements are slow, like he's numb from the cold or from blood loss or both.

"I think we have to find shelter," he tells Dawn, and his voice is scary weak, and he can't meet her eyes.

Dawn looks around at the barren rock and doesn't see how shelter is possible. "Where?" she asks.

Lucas rubs his forehead. "I think I saw a little protected alcove back there," he tells her. "It should keep us out of the wind, anyway."

It's their only hope, Dawn knows. They can't stay out here any longer. Now that they're not moving, the cold's really settling in: bitter, life-sapping cold, blasted into their faces by an unrelenting wind.

And it's clear that Lucas can't make it much farther.

She nods, weakly. Turns around. "Let's go."

Fifteen minutes later, they're huddled inside a shallow crevice, shielded from the wind on three sides by the rock. Dawn lets Lucas go first and then crowds in behind him, and the gap in the rock isn't quite deep enough to fit them both, so she still feels the wind at her back as she squeezes in and crouches beside him. Still, it's marginally warmer here, and if they huddle together, they can probably survive the night.

Dawn lies there and shivers and feels Lucas shivering beside her. It's not windy in this little crevice but it's open at the top and the temperature is still falling. Their clothes are wet and they're on top of a mountain.

And Dawn is so tired but she can't fall asleep, not until her mind has forced her to think about all of the things that have gone wrong.

Like, from the very beginning.

From the moment she killed her dad.

That's what Dawn thinks about, lying there in the cold.

89.

DAWN DIDN'T KILL HIM ON PURPOSE.

(Duh.)

But it's her fault that he's dead.

It's her fault and she lives with it and it comes back and haunts her, and that's why she gets stoned and fucked up so much, because it's only when she's fucked up that the guilt goes away.

There are no pills on this mountain, and no whiskey or gin.

There's just guilt.

And the cold.

90.

HOW IT HAPPENED WAS STUPID.

She'd gone to the movies with her two best friends, Madison and Olivia. They went to the late showing of the most recent Avengers.

It was supposed to be a girls' night and they were supposed to stay over at Madison's house afterward, but Olivia knew these guys who were having a party, including this one guy, Scott, who was a little bit older and a little bit of a d-bag and who had way more than a little bit of a thing for Olivia.

So they went to the party.

The party wasn't much of a party.

The party was Scott and his two sketchy friends playing video games in Scott's basement and stealing pulls from a bottle of Jameson. Dawn walked into that basement and took one look at the boys and figured out it wasn't really her scene.

But she kept her mouth shut, because Olivia liked Scott.

And Dawn didn't want to seem like the lame one in the group.

(Dawn was like fourteen at this point.)

(She'd had—*maybe*—a wine cooler or two at this point in her drinking career.)

(She'd never gone shot for shot over whiskey with three boys who were bigger and older than her. But she tried—oh, she tried—and it wasn't long before Dawn was quite shit-faced.)

It was at this point that the party began to break up. Olivia paired off with Scott and disappeared to his room. Madison and this other guy, Ryan, started making out on the couch.

That left Dawn, and contestant No. 3—and it's a testament to that Jameson that Dawn doesn't even remember his name.

(Nor does she really remember how she wound up on top of him.)

What Dawn does remember, though, is that—before things got too heavy—she threw up. It was gross. It was whiskey and movie popcorn and, like, M&M's. Plus Wendy's famous tuna casserole and the school cafeteria's mystery meat.

And it was *everywhere*.

Needless to say, that put a dent in the party.

Contestant No. 3 immediately fell out of love. Scott threw a fit. And Dawn decided it was probably in her best interest to leave.

Now, Dawn's father was a sensible parent.

"I know there are going to be parties when you get to high school," he'd told Dawn and Bryce. "And I know that some kids are going to experiment with alcohol."

(He said it in that dad way where it's immediately uncool and mortifying, but the message was on point.)

"I just want you to know," he told Dawn and Bryce, "that if you're ever stranded somewhere and you need a ride home, we'll come get you."

"No questions, no judgment," he told Dawn and Bryce. "Anytime, day or night."

91.

IF SHE'D CALLED for a taxi, Dawn would still have a father. If she'd taken the bus, or just crashed on Scott's front steps. If she hadn't had so much whiskey, and just been a good daughter.

If she'd done literally anything else, her dad would still be alive.

92.

DAWN'S FATHER Did the Right Thing.

Without hesitation.

He answered the phone when Dawn called him, and he told her he'd be there to get her in a couple of minutes, and he ended the call and picked up his car keys and set out to find her.

He didn't find Dawn.

He never made it to Scott's house.

The police told Dawn and Wendy and Bryce that the guy who ran the red light had a blood alcohol concentration more than twice the legal limit.

They told Wendy her husband was dead in an instant.

The other driver walked away from the crash and straight into the back of a Sacramento PD cruiser.

He went to jail for a while, but he's alive.

Dawn never saw her father again.

Except on nights like this, when she's guilty.

And she doesn't have anything strong enough to chase the guilt away.

93.

EVENTUALLY, DAWN FALLS ASLEEP.

It takes a long time and she's not even sure how it happens, and it's likely she wouldn't even realize she'd fallen asleep except that something happens to make Dawn suddenly very conscious of the fact she's awake.

Like she was lying there in a dream state of cold and wetness, some kind of trance, without ever realizing she'd drifted off.

It's only when she comes back to the crevice that Dawn realizes she was gone.

Because wherever Dawn was a few moments ago, she was there alone. In her head, in her thoughts.

(With her dad.)

She'd forgotten about Lucas; he was elsewhere.

But he's here now.

He's here, and he's in a bad spot.

And Dawn's instantly awake.

94.

LUCAS ISN'T BREATHING RIGHT. And not in the way that guys sometimes do when they're passed out asleep and snoring like a bear or, like, an eighteen-wheeler.

That's annoying, but it's not, you know, concerning.

Dawn wakes up because she realizes that Lucas isn't moving. And she listens and she can't hear him breathing over the sound of the wind, and then she panics and starts to believe he might be dead, and she reaches for him in the dark and finds his face and his neck and feels around for a pulse.

And his pulse is there, but it's weak.

And when she turns on her flashlight and shines the light at him she can see he's breathing, but it's super shallow. And then every now and then he'll, like, gasp really loud and suck in a mouthful of air like he's dying, and his face will contort and she can see he's in pain.

And she can see all the blood that's leaked out through the hole in his jacket.

Dawn points the flashlight beam at the rock wall. Props it up there so it will stay and she'll have both her hands free.

Lucas is curled up on his side with his legs bent. Gingerly, Dawn tries to roll him a little bit. She reaches for the zipper on his jacket.

Lucas stirs, but he doesn't wake up. It's so cold in the little crevice but his skin is hot to her touch, too hot. He whimpers a little bit as she unzips his jacket. But he doesn't wake up, and Dawn doesn't know if that's a good thing or not.

There's so much blood underneath.

He was wearing a T-shirt to sleep in, and that's all he has on underneath his jacket. He's a Black Bear, so the T-shirt is red, but it's a bright cherry red. It's nothing like the deep crimson staining his midsection.

The fabric is slashed open, just above Lucas's belly button. His whole stomach is sticky with blood, some of it dried and some of it fresh. Some of it has soaked through the shirt, gluing the fabric to his skin. Dawn stares at the stab wound and feels sick to her stomach.

Lucas whimpers again. It's the noise a child would make, or maybe a sick animal. It's pain and fear and exhaustion.

Dawn zips his jacket back up, to the top. Then she turns off the flashlight and sits there in the dark, her back to the storm, straining her ears to listen to Lucas breathing.

⸻

Time passes. Dawn can't say how long, only that she lies there and listens to the wind and feels Lucas breathing softly, and every now and then he'll wake up and gasp a lungful of air again, and he'll cry out from the pain of moving and his breathing afterward will be hot and fast and feverish.

He's in bad shape; that much is obvious.

And sooner or later, Dawn realizes that she can't ask him to go any farther.

"Lucas," she says. She turns on the flashlight. *"Lucas, wake up."* She shines the light on him. He doesn't open his eyes. He's shivering now, from the cold or from something else entirely.

"Lucas," Dawn says. She shakes him, gently, and watches his forehead furrow. He stirs a little bit, but doesn't open his eyes.

"Hmm?" he says, finally.

"Lucas, I think you're hurt," Dawn tells him. "Like, really bad."

Lucas doesn't answer immediately. He exhales, and it sounds ragged. "Yeah," he says. His voice is weak. "Warden got me."

He shifts a little bit, and Dawn sees how every muscle in his face goes tense with the effort and the pain of moving. And she can see the blood staining the front of his red Black Bear jacket and she wonders how he even made it this far, how he didn't just drop dead hours before.

"I don't think . . . I can do this," Lucas says, and that scares her. It scares her because she knows how bad Lucas wants to play the hero, how he wants to be the one who saves the day.

Solid and dependable.

"I think," Lucas says, "I think I just need to lie here for a while.

"Dawn," Lucas says. "Are you as scared as I am?"

95.

DAWN'S OUT OF THE CREVICE before she knows what she's doing. She's fifty feet away before she knows that she's gone.

She's left Lucas as comfortable as she can manage. As warm and dry as he's going to get on this ridge. She's left him with nearly all of the food—not that there's much. He's got enough, Dawn figures, to last a day.

She's not sure he'll survive longer than that. Not if she can't find help.

She's lucky she doesn't walk right off that cliff, though. Plummet down into the abyss and die somewhere on the rocks. She's not thinking right, not at all, hyperventilating and her thoughts going supersonic consumed with the idea of saving Lucas. And Amber. And whoever else is still alive.

She's at the edge of the cliff before she realizes she made the wrong turn. Stops, just in time, and turns and hurries back toward the crevice and past it, before she can tell herself she's better off staying put.

Before she can really feel the chill in the air.

Dawn passes the crevice and for a second she thinks she hears Lucas call her name from inside it. He sounds breathless and weak and she wants to go back to him, to lie with him and comfort him, to keep him warm and pretend she's not afraid.

But he'll die on this ridge unless she keeps moving.

Unless she can somehow get him help.

Dawn keeps running, keeps moving. Picks her way across the ridge, away from the crevice and the abyss behind it. Back as best she can figure toward the trail. Toward Brandon and Evan.

Toward Warden, and whatever he has planned.

She's walked about a hundred yards before the adrenaline wears off and the cold really hits her.

The cold bites at Dawn's face and the wind whips through her jacket, and Dawn shakes from the chill and it only gets worse when she stops moving. Her legs and her feet ache and her whole body is exhausted. There's no visibility beyond the beam of her flashlight, no help coming for her, no rescue.

Dawn is hungry and her body is weak.

She stumbles over the rocks and forces herself onward, up the spine of the ridge with no sense of where she's going or where she's even standing, where she exists in the grand scheme of the world.

There is rock and there is night and she moves across

both and she can see the blood all over Lucas's jacket when she closes her eyes and it's enough to keep propelling her forward.

She's not going back there.

She's not letting him die.

96.

BUT LUCAS MIGHT DIE ANYWAY, Dawn knows.

She might, too.

She's numb from the cold and the hunger and the fatigue. Her thoughts slow to sludge and her body won't respond to basic commands. She falls and scrapes her palms on the rocks and lies there and the wind whistles over her and it would be so easy to just close her eyes and sleep.

Dawn lies there and even the cold doesn't seem so bad anymore. Even the rocks seem comfortable beneath her. She could drift away, here, and it might even be pleasant. Dawn closes her eyes and it feels good and nourishing, and she knows if she keeps them closed much longer she won't ever feel the cold again.

Her body feels like it weighs three hundred pounds. Just pushing herself to a sitting position is a chore; standing again is a serious job. Dawn's head is swimming by the time she's upright. She's afraid she might faint.

The wind seems to redouble its efforts to freeze her to

death. Or, barring that, knock her back over, where she'll maybe decide to sleep this time.

Dawn stands in place for a minute, trying to blink away the hunger and the exhaustion. It does marginal good.

She forces herself to start walking again. The beam of her flashlight illuminates the ground just ahead of her, and Dawn knows there isn't a trail to follow and that she's pushing forward on faith.

She knows Brandon and Evan and Warden are out there, waiting for her, and that they'll kill her as sure as the wind will, if they find her.

She knows her odds are slim and she'll probably die, but she knows that Lucas is depending on her. And Amber, who is compassionate and caring and who would be doing the same thing, Dawn knows, not only for her but for any of the kids in her group, no matter what they thought of her.

She makes it another ten, fifteen minutes. Pitch dark and uneven ground, the burn of her muscles as the ridge rises and falls beneath her.

And then Dawn slips again. Misjudges a step and plummets down a bare rock face. It's only ten feet, but when she hits, she hits hard. Twists her ankle on something and batters her arm. Loses her headlamp somewhere and watches the beam blink out.

She tries to stand and nearly screams from the pain. Tries to hobble and just straight collapses. And knows, as she hits the ground, that this is it. There's no more pushing forward. Not on this ankle. Not like this.

This time, it doesn't feel so seductive, the thought of falling asleep. Of dying here on the mountain and never again being cold.

This time, Dawn wants to keep going. For Amber and Lucas. For herself.

She just can't.

She just straight freaking can't.

97.

DAWN DOESN'T DIE ON THAT RIDGE.

She doesn't even have a particularly uncomfortable night, not after she passes out at the base of that fall.

Dawn spends the night clueless, in a state of blissful unconsciousness. Things happen while she's out, but she's not privy to any of it.

And then she wakes up, and the sun is shining and the terrain doesn't quite look as alien and foreboding as it did last night. And then Dawn shifts her weight a little bit and she realizes she's wrapped up in somebody's sleeping bag.

She's warm.

And mostly dry.

And that *somebody* who owns the sleeping bag is watching her carefully.

It's Brielle.

98.

THE BLACK BEAR SITS on a rock across a small clearing from Dawn. She has her big hiking pack beside her, half full or a little less. She doesn't look as tired or, you know, *gaunt* as Lucas did, or Dawn feels. She looks like she's spent some time in the woods, sure, but she doesn't look like she's about to die from it. She looks like she could go another week or so, easy.

Wordlessly, Brielle hands Dawn a granola bar, which Dawn devours. She's so hungry she can barely tear the wrapper open, but she gets it done, and gets it down.

Brielle hands her another bar. "Last one," she says. "For now. We have a long day ahead of us."

Dawn eats the second bar slower, but not by much. Slow enough that she can taste the chocolate chips, anyway. When she's done, she stuffs the wrapper away. "How did you find me?" she asks.

Brielle shrugs. The expression on her face is still inscrutable. It's impossible to tell what she's thinking, about Dawn or the situation or, like, life in general. "Your flashlight," she tells Dawn. "I saw the beam. You know you're on the wrong ridge, right?"

Dawn nods. "Warden kicked over the cairns," she says. "It got dark. We got lost."

Brielle's expression softens, just a tad. "You could have died," she says.

Dawn says, "I'm still not sure I didn't."

According to Brielle, Dawn made it nearly all the way back to the main ridge before she took her little tumble. Hence why Brielle was able to see the beam from her flashlight— and why Brandon and Evan and Warden may have seen the same.

"I followed them out of camp," Brielle tells Dawn. "Yesterday morning. After you and Lucas turned back."

Brielle looks at her. "That was pretty brave," she says. "Going up against Warden like that."

Dawn looks away. "I couldn't just let him get away with murdering Alex and Christian," she says. "No matter how much I wanted to escape."

She closes her eyes. Feels tired and weak, despite the food, despite the rest. Feels overwhelmed by what lies out there waiting for them, by the magnitude of what's left to do.

Brielle snaps her fingers. Dawn opens her eyes.

"Wake up," Brielle says. "We gotta go. I don't know where the boys are, but they're bound to be somewhere close."

Dawn doesn't say anything. She listens instead, to the

sound of the mountain. Hears wind, and nothing else. Nothing that suggests Brandon and Evan and Warden are nearby. But they're out there, Dawn knows. And Lucas's clock is ticking.

Amber's is, too. . . .

99.

ACCORDING TO BRIELLE, Kyla joined Warden and the boys in the pursuit.

"She didn't look, like, *happy* about it," Brielle tells Dawn. "But it's not like she was going to make it to the highway without Warden, either."

"But what about you?" Dawn asks. "Weren't they worried about leaving you behind?"

Brielle shoots her another look. "People don't notice me," she says. "I mean, I'm sure Warden did, but the others? I bet they couldn't even tell you my name."

She'd hidden, she said, when she heard Dawn and Lucas fighting with Warden, and managed to stay hidden as Brandon and Evan riled themselves up for the chase, and after the four Pack members disappeared back up the snowy trail, she'd come out of hiding and gathered what she could and set out to follow.

"No offense," Brielle says, "but I really didn't give you and Lucas much hope of getting back to headquarters, not in a storm. But I knew Warden would probably think I left with you, and the others would just forget about me, so I thought I could slip past and, you know, get to safety, while the rest of you fought it out."

She speaks matter-of-factly, as though this kind of life-or-death disaster is what she normally does for fun, as though two people aren't already dead and more people want to murder each other.

As though she isn't talking about leaving Dawn and Lucas to fend for themselves.

But then she kind of smiles at Dawn. "Anyway, I'm glad I found you," she says. "I didn't really want you to die."

* * *

They pack up and head out.

It's an overcast morning and the ridge is covered in fresh snow, but there's more visibility than yesterday, at least. Dawn can see the spur ridge stretched out in front of them to where it meets the real ridge in the distance. Behind them, somewhere, is the end of the spur ridge, and Lucas.

Dawn tells Brielle about Lucas as they hike. Her ankle is sore, but if she moves slow, she can limp across the rocks on it. Brielle watches her, stays close to Dawn like she's worried she'll fall again, and Dawn wonders why the other girl doesn't just abandon her.

But Brielle isn't going anywhere apparently, so Dawn tells her about Lucas and the spur ridge and the crevice in the rock and the blood. How Lucas was stabbed and it's not only Amber they have to try to save now, but him, too.

And Brielle listens with a grim expression, and when Dawn is at the part where she slips and falls and breaks her flashlight, Brielle glances back once more across the terrain toward the end of the spur ridge and shakes her head.

"What a clusterfuck," she says, and at this point, Dawn is inclined to agree with her.

"You said you left after Warden and the boys," Dawn says, after they've walked a ways in silence. "But I guess you didn't find them."

"Not yet," Brielle replies.

Dawn looks south along the solid spine of rock that marks the trail, two or three more miles over jutting mounds of snowy rock. "Then they're still out there," she says, and she shivers but it's not from the cold. "Ahead of us."

There's nothing to do but move cautiously.

Brielle and Dawn turn their coats inside out so that the bright colors are muted somewhat against the fresh snow. It's probably pointless; the rest of the world is white and gray, and Dawn's coat is yellow and Brielle's is bright blue, but they do it anyway, and they try to stay low as they hurry across the top of the ridge.

The Raven's Claw is behind them now, north. Headquarters is south. Warden and the others are no doubt south already. They hope.

Dawn isn't sure what Brielle plans to do if they see Warden and the others. Hide, probably; Brielle doesn't seem like a fighter. Dawn supposes they'll cross that proverbial bridge when they come to it.

(But you already know they're going to come to that bridge.)

In the meantime, she tries to focus on the hike: one foot in front of the other, watch that tender ankle, that slippery snow. Follow Brielle and try to keep quiet, stop every now and then to scan the ridge up ahead and behind for signs of life.

It's weird, but Dawn doesn't feel as desperate, not with Brielle here. The Black Bear seems to know what she's doing, and she doesn't seem afraid. She shoulders her hiking pack and picks out the trail for them to follow, and Dawn looks out at the ridge ahead of them and can see where in the distance it drops down from the alpine, where the trail will begin again in earnest, back to headquarters.

There is still no sign of Warden and the others, not even fresh tracks in the snow. The mountain is quiet; even the wind has died down some. It's almost peaceful, if you don't think about the murderous psychos on the loose.

After a while, they stop for a rest and a quick snack of hydration candies before they keep going. The sun's obscured by clouds, and Dawn's from the city and couldn't figure out the time anyway, but it still feels like early morning, even though they've been hiking awhile.

"Why are you here?" Dawn asks Brielle.

Brielle hands Dawn her canteen. "What do you mean?" she replies. "I told you, I'm going to headquarters. Someone has to save Amber."

"No, I know that part," Dawn replies. "I mean, why are you *here?* The program? What are you in for?"

Brielle sucks on her candy and doesn't reply for a moment. She looks out across the ridge and down toward the snowy forest below.

"Let's just say my parents and I have fundamentally different opinions about certain aspects of who I am," she says, finally.

Dawn stares at her, not really getting it.

"They're pretty religious," Brielle explains. "I'm . . . not. They thought that sending me here would convert me."

"To a religious person?" Dawn asks.

"No," Brielle says. "To a *straight* one."

Dawn frowns. Brielle catches her expression, and for the first time, Dawn thinks the other girl looks unsure of herself.

Just as quickly, though, Brielle's expression hardens. She closes up again. "I don't want to talk about it," she says.

"It's cool," Dawn says. "I didn't mean—"

"I know it's cool," Brielle replies. "Thank you. End of discussion."

Dawn doesn't say anything. She takes a drink of water and when Brielle reaches for the canteen, Dawn hands it back to her. They stand in silence for a few awkward minutes, Dawn wanting to apologize but afraid of pissing off Brielle more than she has already.

Then Brielle shoulders her pack again. "Come on," she says. "Let's get moving."

"I just," Dawn says.

Brielle stops. Looks at her. "What?"

Dawn hesitates. Can't look at Brielle. "You're going to go back to headquarters," she says. "You're going to turn yourself in."

Brielle says slowly, "Yeah?"

Dawn gestures to Brielle's pack. "You could have gone for the highway," she says. "They'll just send you back to your family."

Brielle doesn't say anything for a beat. Just looks out across the forest some more.

"Amber needs saving," she says, finally. "Lucas, too. I'll deal with my family later."

Then she turns and walks away.

100.

"I KILLED MY DAD," Dawn tells Brielle. She's hurrying to catch up with the other girl, feeling like she has to say something, confess something, to evaporate the awkwardness between them. "I messed up, and my dad died, and that's why they sent me here."

Brielle stops walking. Turns back and looks Dawn over, appraising her. "Explain," she says.

So Dawn explains. About Olivia and Madison and Avengers. About the party and how she'd puked and had to call her dad. About how her dad had come to get her, and how the drunk driver had run the red light. And how it was Dawn's fault, all of it.

It feels good to talk about it. To confess.

And then Dawn tells Brielle the rest, what came after. How she couldn't cope with the grief or the guilt. How she began to cut class, how she began to self-medicate.

How her mom met someone new, and Dawn ran off with Julian.

"None of it would have happened," she tells Brielle, "if I hadn't killed my dad."

Brielle shakes her head. Her lip curls. "That's stupid," she says. "You're not here because you killed your dad. Your dad's death was an accident."

Dawn starts to argue. Brielle cuts her off. "You're here because you don't know how to cope. Because you chose drugs and some asshole named Julian instead of dealing with your feelings like an adult," she says.

Brielle says, "But you didn't kill your dad."

"And you already know that," she says.

Dawn stares at Brielle. She doesn't say anything.

Brielle meets her eyes and just shrugs. "Real talk," she says. "Sorry. But you know who is a killer?"

Beat.

"Warden," Brielle says. "And probably Brandon and Evan, too. And if we don't keep moving, we're going to be their next victims."

101.

IT TURNS OUT BRIELLE is from the same part of Oregon as Warden. It turns out she knows a little bit more about Warden than Dawn. And it turns out Warden wasn't exactly truthful when he was telling Dawn his Origin Story.

"It was in the news," Brielle tells Dawn. "All over the place. I can't believe they let him into this program."

Dawn frowns, confused. "What do you mean?" she asks. "I thought he just . . . stole a truck, or something?"

Brielle makes a face. "He's dangerous," she says. "Like, violent, but you know that. Pretty much the whole county wanted him thrown in jail." She shrugs. "Rich family, though. They talked the judge out of it. Sent him here instead of jail, and now here we are."

Dawn takes a moment to digest this. "Okay," she says. "But what did he do?"

Brielle meets her eyes. "He attacked some guy," she tells Dawn. "Warden and his friends. Beat him nearly unconscious and left him by the side of the ocean." She shakes her head again. "The guy drowned when the tide came in. Warden's friends went to jail."

Brielle shrugs again.

"Rich family," she says again.

There's no time to process this new nugget of information. Not with Warden at large and Amber and Lucas both getting closer to death with every minute that passes.

(Assuming they're not dead already.)

Dawn and Brielle stop talking. They focus on covering ground. It's easy now, in the daylight, with decent visibility and the top of the ridge more or less a straight line, albeit a line with plenty of ups and downs, over boulders and small rises, and down into narrow valleys.

They move slowly, and it's not just because of Dawn's ankle. Warden and the others are out here somewhere, and Dawn knows the last thing she and Brielle need is to stumble upon them accidentally. Ideally, she and Brielle will be able to just dodge the others completely, find a way to sneak past them and continue down to headquarters without Warden or anyone else even realizing they're there. It sounds like the easiest solution to the Warden problem, and given the latest developments, it honestly might be the *only* solution.

There's no way Dawn and Brielle are going to overpower three big teenage boys (plus Kyla, wherever she stands).

So they hike, and hike cautiously, scanning the ridge ahead of them and stopping every few minutes to listen. They don't hear anything; the ridge is still spooky quiet, and so they keep going and hope that, I don't know, Warden and the others fell to their deaths somewhere in the night.

(It feels weird to Dawn to be hoping that other people are dead or at least grievously injured, but whenever she starts to feel guilty she pictures Alex all beaten up and bruised at the bottom of that ravine, and she knows Brandon and Evan will gladly do the same to her if they catch her. It's kill or be killed at this point.)

Dawn and Brielle hike for an hour or so. They climb over the last mini mountain on the top of the ridge, and then the ridge turns southeast and begins to drop altitude, and from what Dawn can remember this means there's only maybe another hour or two in the alpine before they pick up the trail again through the forest.

And after that it's another solid five or six hours, maybe, back to headquarters, but they're traveling light and there's plenty of daylight left, and even though the trail is going to take them right past the spot where that angry mama bear tried to attack her on the outbound hike, Dawn isn't thinking about that right now. She's starting to believe that even on her busted ankle they can make it back, past Warden and the others and even that scary bear; they can make it to safety before darkness sets in.

It's a good thought and it buoys her spirits and gives her energy, and she keeps hiking, following Brielle and putting one foot in front of the other and blocking out the pain and the fatigue and the hunger. They chew up the trail and now and then there's even a cairn again, and even knowing that Warden and the others are out there, Dawn can't help feeling just a little bit optimistic.

She's survived the ridge, and it could have killed her. She didn't freeze to death or plummet into the abyss, and Brandon and Evan didn't catch her. Hiking, in daylight, with Brielle, everything seems safer somehow.

Dawn's even starting to think about what will happen when they reach headquarters, when Brielle stops dead in front of her, and Dawn nearly runs her over.

"Hold up," Brielle says. She's staring at the ground. Dawn looks over Brielle's shoulder, and sees what Brielle sees.

Footprints.

102.

THERE'S JUST ENOUGH SNOW HERE that the footprints show up clearly. They're muddled, some of them—most of them. You'd expect that from a group all following the same trail. But here and there are distinct prints in the snow. Various sizes, but mostly large sizes, boys' sizes—and they're all headed in one direction: east.

"We're still behind them," Brielle tells Dawn. "So that's good."

Dawn stares down at the footprints and knows this gives them a serious advantage. So long as there are prints to follow, they'll know where the boys are. That means they probably won't get ambushed, at least if they're careful.

It's a good sign, but it's spooky, too. It's a clear sign the boys are out here.

Still looking for Dawn and Brielle and Lucas.

Somewhere between here and safety.

Dawn and Brielle follow the footprints.

Well, they follow the ridge and keep the footprints in sight, making sure the prints don't wander off or deviate or circle back or do anything else unexpected.

The prints lead where Dawn and Brielle are heading, down the ridge as it loses altitude and toward the southeast end where it drops into the forest. It's more sheltered here, on this end of the ridge; it's still bare rock and minimal trees and shrubs, but the wind is coming from the west, and so as Dawn and Brielle descend, the ridge forms a natural barrier behind them. It's warmer, marginally. The snow thins out a little bit.

Dawn thinks about Lucas. She wonders if he'll be okay, and for a moment she feels guilty that she abandoned him. Feels like maybe she should have stayed with him, left Brielle to save the day.

He's alone back there, after all. He could have frozen to death in the night, or bled out from the stab wound.

Lucas could be dead, and it would be Dawn's fault.

Just like her dad.

Right?

Brielle stops walking again. This time, Dawn doesn't nearly run her over.

But this time, Brielle doesn't look quite so confident.

She looks back at the trail behind them, then stands on her tiptoes and cranes her neck toward the end of the ridge, a couple of hundred yards away. She frowns and looks around, to the right, where the ridge drops away into a vast, forested valley. And to the left, where it climbs to a stubby summit a few hundred feet above them.

"What?" Dawn asks, the look on Brielle's face starting to scare her. "What is it?"

Brielle doesn't answer right away. She gestures to the ground in front of them. Dawn follows her eyes and sees pristine snow, and for a half second, she doesn't quite get it. Then she does. "The tracks," she says.

Brielle nods, grim. The tracks they've been following, the footprints they were so sure meant Warden and the others were still ahead of them?

They're gone.

Disappeared without any kind of warning. Ended right here on a flat patch of smooth rock, as if at random.

They're just gone.

Dawn stares down at the snow, trying to process it. Her exhausted brain can't figure out what it means. And then Brielle stiffens beside her, and Dawn senses movement in her peripheral vision.

And she turns just in time to see Warden step out from behind a massive boulder, ten or maybe twenty feet back the way they've come. Brandon and Evan flank him, grinning like a couple of maniacs.

(Kyla follows the boys. Reluctantly, from the looks of it.)

(She's not smiling anyway.)

Warden doesn't look quite so crazy as Brandon and Evan. But Dawn can see the glint in those green eyes. He meets her gaze, and his lips curl into a smirk. She can tell he's savoring this.

"Gotcha," he says.

103.

BRIELLE TAKES OFF. Drops her pack and starts running, without a word. Warden glances at Brandon, and Brandon and Evan launch themselves after her, blowing past Dawn like she isn't even there, looking like a couple of hyenas chasing down lunch.

Warden doesn't move, and neither does Dawn. Neither does Kyla for that matter, but Dawn isn't worried about her, not just yet.

She's just hoping that Brielle can get away.

Warden studies Dawn and looks pleased with himself. "We spotted you coming," he says, gesturing over his shoulder up the ridge to the northwest, the way they've come down. "A long way back."

Dawn wishes she could smack the cocky grin right off his face, but she doesn't bother to try.

"Found a nice hiding place," Warden continues. "Then we retraced our steps a little bit, to confuse you." He grins wider. "I guess it worked, huh?"

He takes a step toward her, then another. His eyes don't

leave hers, and the smirk on his face fades into something else. Something . . . remorseful.

"I wish you hadn't run," he tells her. "I *really* wish you hadn't run, Dawn."

He's going to kill her.

A million cliché lines from a million cliché movies run through Dawn's head.

(You'll never get away with this.)

(You don't have to do this.)

(Just let us go; we won't tell on you.)

(I (*sob*) trusted you.)

(Whyyyy?)

But as exhausted and hopeless as Dawn is feeling, it's not enough to send her into full cliché mode, not yet. She's not going to fall for Warden's charm, either, or wish things were different or even feel dumb about possibly falling for him. She's not that girl anymore.

Those days are over.

Dawn looks at Warden and doesn't even notice those green eyes or the obvious muscle beneath his jacket. She doesn't see a busted love triangle when she sees him.

She sees an asshole.

She stands there and looks at him and doesn't say anything, and just hopes that Brielle can get away.

104.

BUT BRIELLE DOESN'T GET AWAY. Brandon and Evan drag her back to where Warden and Dawn and Kyla stand. It's taken a disappointingly short amount of time for them to capture her.

Like, less than ten minutes.

Brielle struggles against them and swears and generally makes it known she doesn't appreciate this treatment. But Brandon and Evan are bigger than her and they grip her tight, and no matter how hard Brielle fights, she can't get away.

(Evan does have a bloody nose, though.)

(And Brandon appears to be limping.)

Brandon and Evan march Brielle to where the others are standing, and they present her to Warden with undisguised pride. And Warden looks at both Dawn and Brielle, and Dawn can see how he's so in love with the idea of himself that he's going to force them to listen to him talk before he kills them.

And at this point, Dawn figures she would probably just prefer death. "Just fucking do it already," she says, before Warden can open his mouth. "Whatever you're planning, spare us the monologue and just get it done."

Warden blinks.

Looks surprised.

Looks almost human. (For a fraction of a second.)

Then his eyes narrow. "Fine," he says. "Let's get it done."

Evan keeps holding Brielle as Brandon comes over to Dawn. He takes her by the shoulders, rough, and grips her so she can feel his fingers through the material of her jacket.

He leans in close to her and Dawn can smell sweat and dirt and *boy*, unwashed hair and unbrushed teeth, and even though she knows she must smell nearly as bad, somehow Brandon's stench seems like the olfactory manifestation of who he is as a person. Which is to say, *foul*.

Noxious.

Evil.

Dawn can feel his stank breath in her ear and she knows he must be grinning, knows he's enjoying this, and she tries to ignore him and tries not to feel scared and pretty well fails at both objectives.

Then Warden tilts his head toward the south edge of the ridge, where it drops into the valley, and Brandon shoves Dawn forward and Evan shoves Brielle, and Dawn realizes the boys mean to throw her and Brielle off the edge of the cliff.

She realizes this is it.

105.

"KYLA," DAWN SAYS when Warden's led them to the edge of a precipice that doesn't seem nearly as high as the abyss into which Dawn and Lucas nearly plummeted last night, but is still plenty high enough to kill them.

(And is studded with jagged rocks.)

(And trees.)

(And other painful obstacles.)

"Kyla," she says, and hates how shaky and desperate she sounds. "Kyla, are you seriously *okay* with this?"

She twists around in Brandon's grip to meet the other girl's eyes, but Kyla won't look at her. Stares down at the ground instead. "I'm sorry," she says. "I just can't go back where I came from."

"They're going to kill us," Dawn tells her. "You know that, right?"

Kyla doesn't answer.

"You think I want to go home?" Dawn says. "My life's a fucking mess, Kyla. I live with a drug dealer. You think I want to go back?"

Kyla still doesn't answer.

"I *wish* I could still run away," Dawn says. "You think I don't want to just follow you out to that highway and disappear and start over?"

"I do," Dawn says. "I really freaking do. But here's the thing. I'm not a fucking *murderer*, Kyla. I can't just fucking *kill* someone to get what I want."

"Kyla," Dawn says.

"You're not a murderer either."

"Don't you let them *do* this."

Dawn is too angry at Kyla to be scared. Like, she knows she's probably going to die anyway, but it pisses her off that Kyla's just going to go along with it. Like, *Grow some backbone, girl.*

Like, at least lodge a complaint.

But Kyla doesn't do anything, not one token gesture. She just wipes her eyes and looks out across the valley. "I'm so sorry," she says again.

Then she walks away, and that's when Dawn knows she and Brielle are properly, truly fucked.

She knows that in a minute or so, Warden is going to tell Brandon and Evan to push her and Brielle over the edge of this cliff. And she'll fall, and Brielle will fall, and they'll collide into those jagged rocks and be impaled by trees and by the time they hit bottom they'll be barely recognizable.

And when the rescue teams finally come and find their bodies—assuming they even find the bodies before spring—it's going to look, by and large, like two silly girls had a terrible accident, not that they were horribly murdered.

And Warden and Brandon and Evan and Kyla will be long gone by then, disappeared into the ether, and Brielle and Dawn and Lucas and Alex and Christian and Amber will just be six casualties in a terrible, terrible catastrophe.

Dawn can see it play out.

And even if she doesn't have the details quite right, what she's one hundred percent sure of is that Brandon is going to push her over the edge of this cliff.

And she's going to fall.

And she's going to die.

106.

(OF COURSE, THIS ISN'T TRUE.

You know that's not how this story ends.

And you've maybe even figured out how Dawn and Brielle are going to extricate themselves from this sticky, *shitty* situation.

That's right.

Our old buddy, Lucas.)

107.

THIS IS THE MOMENT Lucas has been waiting for his whole life, if we're being perfectly honest.

He's managed to track Dawn and Brielle down the ridge to this very moment, the last possible seconds before their terrible deaths, limping, bleeding, exhausted, and as he hides behind a boulder a few feet away, Lucas knows his time is now.

(It had damn well better be.)

He listens to Dawn try to reason with Kyla. He recognizes pretty quick that it's not going anywhere. He leans down and fumbles in the snow and comes up with the only weapon he can find.

(A large rock.)

He hefts it. Tests its weight.

And then, before Warden can tilt his head and give Brandon and Evan permission to do the thing . . .

Lucas steps out to save the day.

108.

DAWN HEARS A CRAZY kamikaze scream from somewhere behind her, and then she hears Warden swear, and then it's like a million different things are happening at the same time and her mind can't even process.

Brandon loosens his grip on Dawn enough that she can turn and see Lucas appearing out of nowhere, holding a rock over his head and staggering toward Warden, his face contorted in, like, a heroic expression.

Everyone stops to look at Lucas—

(except Brielle).

Brielle wrenches free of Evan's grasp—

(there is a brief, desperate struggle)

—and then Evan goes tumbling off the edge of the cliff.

And from the sound he makes when he lands,

Dawn can tell that it hurts.

109.

ALL GOOD, RIGHT?

Except . . .

At exactly the same time as Evan's taking his final flying leap, Warden is sidestepping Lucas's attack and slashing Lucas with the knife again, making Lucas cry out and knocking him to the ground.

Brielle, now free of Evan forever, rushes toward Warden to help Lucas.

This leaves Dawn and Brandon at the edge of the cliff. It leaves Brandon still gripping Dawn's shoulders, both of them teetering on the precipice, above the rocks and the trees and Evan's broken body far below.

The way Brandon's shoving Dawn forward, Dawn can tell he means to send her down after his bestie.

And she's struggling to get free, but Brandon's grip is just too tight.

110.

IT'S LUCAS WHO SEES that Dawn is in trouble.

Lucas, who's doubled over in the snow, grasping his bloody stomach and trying to find a way to force himself to stand up again. Lucas, who looks up and sees how Brandon is trying to maneuver Dawn over the edge of the cliff without falling himself.

And it's Lucas who forgets about the *second* big freaking stab wound he's just sustained and who launches himself up to his feet again toward Brandon and Dawn, intent on saving the day again, only better this time since the last time didn't work out so well.

Dawn doesn't see Lucas coming. But she feels him hit Brandon, feels the breath from Brandon's lungs expel right into her left ear, feels Brandon's legs start to give out and both of them start to fall.

She feels their mutual equilibrium start to teeter over the edge.

And then Brandon lets her go.

Releases her, just like that, and all of a sudden Dawn is

weightless, and she can feel that she's falling and there's no way she can stop it.

Time seems to pause. Dawn hangs there in place. Knowing that at any instant time will restart again and she'll be falling, hard, to her death.

Except . . .

Lucas.

<hr />

Lucas reaches out and grabs her sleeve. Saves her freaking life. He holds on to her jacket with hands slick with blood and he pulls Dawn back over the edge and to solid ground.

But.

In doing so, he opens himself up to a counterattack from Brandon, who seizes the opportunity to shove Lucas out into thin air.

Lucas releases Dawn just before he starts falling.

Dawn stumbles onto the rocks and turns around to help Lucas.

But Lucas is beyond help.

Dawn sees his eyes go wide as he realizes what he's done. Sees his arms reach out and flail for something solid; sees his hands grip Brandon's jacket but fail to hold on.

She sees Lucas disappear over the edge of the cliff.

She screams.

111.

DAWN BLACKS OUT, A LITTLE BIT.

Like, something else takes control of her body. She's not even thinking about killing Brandon, but it happens anyway.

She's just so shook about Lucas.

Brandon's standing there at the edge of the cliff, triumphant, looking down at Lucas falling, and Dawn hears Lucas hit something and it's like someone dropped a couch from the top of a ten-story building.

She realizes that Lucas is probably dead, and then she stops thinking.

She football-rushes Brandon as he turns from the cliff, that shit-eating, hyena grin still plastered on his face. She collides with Brandon with both of her hands outstretched, hits him with her full body weight and sends him flying backward.

Sends him falling off the cliff.

It takes all Dawn has not to go over with him, to slow her

momentum on the slippery rocks and squirm away from his scrabbling hands, but she does it.

She dodges Brandon, and she watches him fall. But she turns away before he hits bottom. She doesn't want to see Lucas down there. Not now.

112.

IF YOU'RE GOOD AT MATH, you'll recognize that leaves four contestants.

Warden and Kyla.

Dawn and Brielle.

Kyla isn't much of a horse in this race. She isn't fighting anyone, anyway; she's just standing off to the side with a look of, like, panic on her face.

A look of, like, *What the fuck have we done?*

Kyla's a noncombatant.

That leaves Dawn and Brielle to take care of Warden. And at any other time, Dawn would be feeling those odds.

Except right now, Brielle is flat on her back in the snow. She's bleeding from somewhere and she isn't moving.

And Warden is standing above her with that big hunting knife.

Brielle is neutralized.

And Warden's turning around to take care of Dawn next.

113.

DAWN VERSUS WARDEN. Warden versus Dawn.

(You had to know this was coming.)

These are not odds that Dawn thinks she can handle. Not faced off with Warden on the edge of a cliff, Warden holding a bloody knife and with murder in his eyes.

Dawn can see the real Warden now, the boy who earned his sentence to Out of the Wild by killing somebody, the boy who hurts people for his own gain and probably enjoys it. The boy who doesn't belong here. Who belongs, like, in jail.

He's not looking at Dawn with that cocky smile anymore. No, he's breathing heavy and looking up at her from underneath a fallen lock of hair, and he's still smiling a little bit but it's beyond any smile Dawn has ever seen or wants to see again.

He's enjoying this, very much.

And he's so looking forward to the thrilling finale.

The whole mountain seems to go still.

There's nowhere to run.

It's fight for your life, and Dawn knows she can't win. She gets ready to fight anyway.

Warden seems impossibly large as he looms over her. The knife in his hand is still stained with Brielle's blood, and Lucas's. He raises it over his head as he closes the distance between them, and Dawn backs up and braces herself and hopes she can dodge him.

But she can't dodge forever.

Warden's smile is gone now. He's five feet away and closing. He swings the knife back and takes aim at her head, and Dawn knows he'll kill her with one swipe if he hits her.

She scrabbles around for something, anything, to protect her.

Her hand comes up empty.

Warden lunges.

114.

BUT WARDEN'S LEGS CRASH OUT from under him before he can slash open Dawn's skull.

He falls to the ground hard and the knife skitters away, and behind him, Dawn can see Kyla, standing there gripping a tree branch like a baseball bat, an *Oh my God, I've fucking done it now* expression on her face.

Even as Dawn and Kyla make eye contact, Warden is scrambling to his feet, swearing and fumbling for the knife.

Kyla hits him again. Then she drops the branch.

Looks at Dawn and says one thing:

"Run."

115.

DAWN RUNS. She doesn't look back. She doesn't know if Kyla keeps hitting Warden or if Warden stabs Kyla or if a UFO lands between the two of them and abducts them to a strange and unfamiliar galaxy.

She doesn't know anything.

She just runs.

Her feet slip in the snow and her busted ankle screams. Her vision tunnels into nothing but the ridge ahead of her and a blur on either side; she zeros in on one merciful cairn standing dead ahead, and scrambles over the rocks toward it.

It's pure adrenaline now.

There's nothing else. Nothing left. Just heart-charging adrenaline and the knowledge that it's death if she so much as slows down.

So she doesn't.

Dawn reaches the first cairn, and then she sees the next, and when she reaches that one, she sees the ridge drop away and the trail snake out before her into the rain forest, and she descends from the ridge at an unsafe speed and somehow manages not to die.

In the blink of an eye she's in the forest and there's snow but not as much as on top, in the alpine, and the trail is visible enough as it cuts through the trees.

There are still miles to go. There are miles and miles to go. Warden is somewhere behind, and Dawn is still running. She runs through the forest and she continues to run, and for a while she doesn't feel tired; she's too scared. She's too aware of how everything now depends on her.

The fear gives her strength.

The strength gives her speed.

Dawn runs down the trail and she doesn't slow down.

116.

DAWN RUNS UNTIL SHE'S SURE her lungs will burst, and then she keeps running.

She runs until her busted ankle feels forever broken and irreversibly ruined, until she can't take a step without the pain bringing fresh tears to her eyes.

And she keeps running.

She runs as the trail winds down through the forest, curling into the subalpine and below, the air getting warmer and the snow disappearing.

She runs until she can't possibly run anymore, and then she runs more.

Dawn runs.

But eventually . . . Dawn stops running.

She's standing beside a small lake. It's a lake she remembers from the hike up. She remembers it because the Pack camped near it on their first night out from headquarters.

She remembers it because of the bear.

Somewhere near this lake is where that pissed-off mama bear found Dawn, and tried to make her dinner. The trail Dawn is following circles around the west side of the lake and then continues its drop through the trees, and somewhere before that drop is where the Pack camped their first night, and where Dawn nearly died.

Dawn didn't plan to stop here. Didn't realize she was stopping until her body ceased to move. It's like she tripped some switch inside herself, some override trigger, and it slammed on the emergency brakes.

And now she stands in the woods on the shore of this lake, breathing so hard she thinks her heart might burst loose from her chest.

And the air is still. No sign of mama bear.

Dawn dares to look behind her. She imagines that Warden is right on her ass, that he'll tackle her from behind and cut her open with that knife and that will be the end of this story.

But Warden isn't behind her. The trail she's run down is empty. It could be that Warden never followed her at all. It could be that angry bear is the only thing standing between Dawn and freedom.

Dawn wishes she could believe that. It would make the next couple of hours of hiking seem a lot shorter.

But she knows Warden's out there.

He has to be.

Stories like this don't just end without that final battle.

And it's funny: a few days ago, that pissed-off mama bear

was the scariest thing Dawn could ever conceive of having to encounter in these woods.

Now? She'll take her chances.

Dawn keeps going.

If the bear is still out there, maybe it will kill Warden instead.

117.

DAWN'S JUST ABOUT at the other end of the lake when she looks back across the water, and that's when she sees Warden.

He's just coming out of the trees on the far shore. He's running, but in that way athletic people sometimes do where it doesn't look like they're expending any effort at all.

Dawn catches herself staring. Like in that sick, fascinated way you would stare at, like, a big hornet. Or a poisonous snake. Or, I don't know, a police car you just blew past at twenty-five over the speed limit.

Like when you know it's dangerous and possibly fatal to just stop and stare, but something triggers in your mind and you can't take your eyes away.

That's how Dawn feels, watching Warden. He runs down to the shore of the lake and then starts along the trail that skirts the water. He is as big and dangerous and unstoppable as any monster in any horror movie. Dawn watches him and knows she should run, but she can't.

She's frozen.

And then Warden looks up and sees her and he starts to run faster.

And suddenly Dawn is unfrozen again.

118.

THE TRAIL DROPS FROM THE LAKE through the forest. It switchbacks down the side of the mountain, and at the bottom is a wider off-road track and if you follow that track for, like, maybe a mile, you'll come to the clearing where the Out of the Wild headquarters waits.

But there are a lot of switchbacks before you reach that track.

Dawn finds her strength again. She starts running. Clear of the lake and down into the forest again. There is no snow here, just wet ferns and moss. Tall trees block out the sun and cast gnarled roots across the trail at irregular intervals.

Dawn follows the trail to the first switchback and pulls a 180 and continues the descent. Her legs are weak and her ankle is sore and somebody is going to have to amputate her knees when all of this is said and done; they're throbbing from the constant pounding, the stress of her body weight colliding with hard earth at a rate of about two collisions per second.

She's so hungry and thirsty that she can't really see.

She's so scared that it doesn't matter.

Dawn hits the second switchback and grabs a tree trunk to swing herself around. Keeps running. Then she hears Warden above her. Crashing through the forest, coming in hot.

Dawn glances back and sees him upslope. He's not on the trail.

He's not using the switchbacks.

Warden's coming down the mountain in a straight line, aiming for Dawn like a guided missile.

He's closing in fast.

So eff the switchbacks.

Dawn veers off the trail and onto the slope. It's steep and wet and littered with fallen trees and stumps and branches. It's impossible to navigate, but somehow Warden is doing it. Dawn knows her only hope is to try to do the same.

She slides down the muddy terrain, trying to avoid downfall and blowdown and all of the other names for fallen trees that she heard Christian and Amber use.

She grabs at living trees as she descends, using them to slow her fall and guide her. She collides into massive trunks hard, her breath stolen from her, bounces off them and keeps dropping. Meets up with the trail again as it switches back and forth, leisurely, but ain't nobody got time for that, not now.

There's no telling how long the drop down the mountain will take, now that Dawn's off-trail again. It's quicker than the switchbacks, anyway. Assuming she can stay upright, which she can't. Not on a ruined ankle and two failing knees. Not exhausted to the point of hallucination. Not on a carpet of mud and roots and loose rock.

Dawn loses her balance. Her arms pinwheel, searching for something to break her fall. Her arms come up empty. She crashes to the earth and tumbles down the steep slope.

The fall fucking sucks.

It hurts like a mother. Over and over and over again. Dawn closes her eyes and tries to protect her head and collides into things and pinballs off them and keeps falling.

She reaches for trees as she passes them and her hands grasp at the earth and come up muddy and it does nothing to arrest her descent.

She knows she'll keep falling until she hits something big, something hard.

Something that might kill her if she hits it hard enough.

There's nothing she can do but continue to fall. And hope that her body can withstand the impact.

119.

DAWN COLLIDES WITH A TREE.

It's massive. It's probably a hundred years old, maybe more. It's been standing in the same place for more than a century, and it sure as hell isn't moving for Dawn.

She crashes into it hard. Like, concussion hard. Black-out-for-a-minute-and-wake-up-confused hard.

Dawn hits and blacks out and then she comes to. Her brain's more or less jelly and she couldn't tell you her last name. All she knows is that she has to keep running. There's a problem, though. She can't.

Dawn's reached her breaking point.

She's tapped out. Exhausted.

Her whole body feels broken and she can't focus her thoughts. Her mind is swimming; she's weak from hunger and exertion and she hurts all over from the fall.

Standing is not an option anymore.

Running? Forget it.

Dawn can barely keep her eyes open.

She can hear Warden up the hillside above her. He's crashing around like a real-life grizzly bear. It's impossible to say how far he is, but Dawn knows he's getting closer.

She knows her only option is to hide and hope that Warden doesn't see her.

But that's not what happens.

120.

DAWN SEES WARDEN up the slope at more or less the same moment Warden sees her.

She can tell that he sees her because he slows down. And smiles.

It's that evil smile again. The real Warden smile.

The smile that says *I've got you, and I'm going to hurt you.*

But something happens at the same time as Dawn sees Warden smile. The same time as Warden begins his slow, steady, victorious descent.

Dawn hears something else, something behind her.

Downslope.

Dawn hears movement.

There's somebody else on the trail.

121.

THERE'S NO POINT in trying to hide anymore. Dawn screams for her life.

"*Help!* Help me, please!"

With every last ounce of strength she can muster, Dawn screams for help.

Above her, Warden continues to descend. He doesn't speed up, and he doesn't slow down. He just drops, slowly and steadily.

And Dawn keeps screaming.

⸻

Whoever it is on the trail?

They hear Dawn.

They stop moving, and then they call back, "Hello?"

A man's voice. A voice Dawn doesn't recognize. But that doesn't matter.

She screams for help again.

⸻

Warden keeps dropping. He's twenty feet away now, and Dawn keeps turning to look up at him and then screaming again. And as he gets closer, she screams louder, more desperate, until it's barely words coming out but just something primal.

It tears her throat raw.

But it doesn't stop Warden. Warden keeps coming. He keeps coming and in Dawn's eyes he's not even close to the boy she thought she could be falling for.

He's a monster.

And her screams don't hurt him.

He's ten feet above her now. Coming down fast. Whoever's on the trail is crashing up through the bushes toward them, but they're too slow, too late; Warden will get to Dawn first.

Dawn looks up at Warden and doesn't even see life anymore in his eyes. Doesn't even see a smile. Just grim, deadly determination. Like a shark.

He's almost on top of her, and Dawn closes her eyes. She stops screaming, even.

It's over.

All she can hope is that Warden kills her quickly.

But then Warden walks past her. She *feels* him brush past as though she isn't even there. Listens as he continues down the slope of the mountain toward the innocent bystander who's coming up toward them, drawn by Dawn's screams, and hoping to help.

Instantly, Dawn knows what Warden is thinking. She's too

exhausted to move, but the bystander is a threat. She knows Warden means to neutralize that threat. She knows once that's over, he'll come back for her.

Dawn starts screaming again. Loud as she can.

This time, she's screaming at the bystander to run.

122.

THE MAN DOESN'T RUN. Not in time, anyway. Dawn hears him say something as Warden appears on the slope above him. She can't make out the words, but his voice is confused.

She can't hear if Warden answers.

She hears the man's voice again and this time it's not confusion she hears, but fear. And then pain. And then she can't hear the man's voice anymore, just the sound of something hard slamming against something soft, over and over and over again.

And then she hears nothing at all.

He'll come back for her now.

Dawn knows this.

She knows the innocent bystander is good and dead, and as soon as Warden is sure of it, he'll come back up the slope to where she's lying here fully spent, and then he'll finish her off.

Maybe fast, or maybe slow.

She looks around for a weapon. There's nothing but soggy

tree branches and soggier mud. There's not even any half-decent rocks.

You can't kill a monster with mud.

Already, Dawn can hear Warden moving back up the slope through the bush. She knows her time on this earth is growing extremely limited.

She knows her only hope is to come for Warden first.

To use her own body as a weapon.

And she knows she has no time to spare.

Just standing up is the most challenging thing Dawn has ever done in her life. Her arms feel like jelly and her legs don't exist, but somehow she manages to pull herself up and lean against that hundred-year-old tree that nearly killed her, and she stays there for a half second to catch her breath and blink the tears from her eyes.

She listens to Warden coming up the slope and knows that he must be only a few feet down from the other side of the tree.

She knows it's time.

She forces her mind to forget about the exhaustion. Pushes off from the tree and steps out from around it, nearly collapsing when she puts her whole weight on her legs.

In fact, she does collapse.

Falls back to the ground and hits so hard she thinks she might die.

But it's not a big deal, Dawn collapsing.

Because when she falls, she takes Warden with her.

123.

WITH THE LAST OF HER STRENGTH, Dawn throws herself down the slope toward Warden. He's off guard, off-balance; he doesn't see her coming. Not until she's in the air, until she's nearly on top of him.

Then his eyes go wide and he puts up his hands to defend himself.

But it's too late. Dawn's coming down, and Warden can't swat her away. She wraps her arms around him and carries him with her, stealing his balance and sending him tumbling backward.

She holds on to him as best as she can as they roll down the slope. But the slope is too steep and they're falling too fast. Sooner or later, they disengage. Uncouple. They tumble down the hillside together, but apart.

Dawn catches a glimpse of something orange on her way down. A glimpse of a face, bloody, eyes open and unseeing.

She knows it must be the bystander and that the bystander is dead.

Then she collides into something and the pain is all-encompassing, and Dawn blacks out again.

124.

SHE WAKES UP ON THE TRAIL. Somehow, they've come to rest on one of the switchbacks.

Dawn can see the dead bystander in his orange jacket fifteen or twenty feet off the trail, upslope. She can see an Out of the Wild logo on his baseball cap. And when she looks closer, she can see it's Steve.

Steve, the guy who picked her up from the airport.

Who brought her into this mess.

Dawn feels no satisfaction at seeing him dead. But she doesn't feel anything else, either. She's just numb.

She lifts her head a little bit and looks around and sees Warden. He lies a few feet from her, on his back, his neck skewed at a crazy angle. He's bleeding.

He's not moving.

But from the rise and fall of his chest, Dawn can tell he's still alive.

She knows this is not a good sign. She's seen too many scary movies to believe this is over. She knows the only way to really end this story is to kill Warden dead and make sure he stays that way.

She doesn't have a weapon, but Warden seems to have dropped his knife, and Dawn knows she could crawl over to him and just, you know, cut off his air supply or something. Crush his windpipe. Something brutal and awful and guaranteed effective.

She has enough strength to kill him. Barely. And Dawn knows that's what has to happen.

But Dawn isn't a killer.

Dawn has done a lot of bad shit in her life.

She's cut class and partied and hooked up with weirdos. She's been rude to her mom and her stepdad and her teachers. She ran away and shacked up with a drug dealer.

She got drunk and threw up on some guy and that's why her father is dead.

If you asked her, Dawn would tell you she's not a good person.

But Dawn isn't a killer.

Not like this.

She shoved Brandon off that cliff, sure, but that was different. That was a fight.

That was him or her.

Warden's unconscious. He doesn't look like a monster anymore. He looks like a teenager. A fragile, broken boy. Dawn can't crush his windpipe.

She can't strangle him to death.

(But you and I both know that's going to come back and bite her.)

125.

THE OUT OF THE WILD GUY, Steve, must have a radio.

That's Dawn's thought. That's her rationalization for not killing Warden. She'll crawl up to the dead guy and take his radio and call for help, and hopefully Warden will stay unconscious or even die on his own.

She won't have to kill him.

That's her plan.

She has to crawl on her stomach and her hands and knees and she's covered in mud by the time she gets up to the dead guy, and her legs are mostly useless, so it's her arms pulling her up the slope, but at this point, Dawn's arms are more or less useless, too.

It takes a long time.

The dead guy lies on his back with his head up the direction of the slope, and Dawn can see how Warden stabbed him a bunch of times and then he must have hit him with a rock for good measure. The dead guy is in fact Steve, and from this angle he doesn't look very old or particularly tough; he looks surprised and, I don't know, offended that Warden actually killed him.

But that doesn't matter now.

What matters is the radio. Dawn finds the handset strapped to the dead guy's belt. It's a little bit bigger than a cell phone, and it looks intact. She pulls it out of the dead guy's holster and fumbles for the on switch.

(She's never used a radio before, but she's hoping if she just starts calling for help someone will figure out the rest.)

Dawn locates the on switch. And the button you push to transmit a message.

She's about to transmit her very desperate message, when—

(you guessed it)

—Warden.

126.

WARDEN GRABS DAWN'S LEG AND PULLS.

He drags her away from the dead guy and down the slope again. He's barely able to stand, hunched over and glaring at her with blood coming down his face, and his neck still skewed in that weird way.

He's favoring his left arm, too, so maybe that's broken. Either way, he looks like he had the shit kicked out of him, and bad, but Dawn knows he's still stronger than her by a mile. She knows that he means to kill her.

He drags her down the slope toward the trail, but this time Dawn isn't too worried. She isn't worried that Warden's stronger than her. She isn't worried that he'll have no problem killing her. She isn't even kicking herself for not crushing his windpipe when he was unconscious.

No, as Warden drags her back down toward the trail, Dawn's actually feeling pretty chill about the whole situation.

Why?

Because Dawn found something more than just the radio when she went up the mountain to the dead guy.

She found Warden's knife, too.

The knife he stole from Christian. That he used on Lucas and Brielle. The knife that's still slick with his sweat, and their blood.

And as Warden drags her down on her stomach and flips her over onto her back on the trail, Dawn grips that knife, tight.

And at just the right moment,

she leans up

and jams that motherfucking blade

right into his chest.

127.

THERE'S NO COMING BACK from that, not even if you're the kind of semi-indestructible final-boss bogeyman who tends to populate stories like these.

But Dawn stabs Warden again, just to be sure.

She stabs him until he staggers away and collapses and lies there on the trail on his back, and she holds on to the knife and watches him and you'd better believe it's a long freaking time that she does, until she's sure he's not moving, not breathing, not playing dead and just waiting for her to turn her back.

Dawn lies there, for maybe an hour or even longer, and Warden doesn't move, and neither does the other dead guy, and the mountain around them is silent.

And then finally, when Dawn's *sure*, she crawls back up the slope for the radio.

AUTHOR'S NOTE

NOW, THIS IS THE PART *where I tell you everything turns out okay. The right people survive, and the main character learns a valuable lesson, and everything is just fairy-tale perfect from here on out.*

But you and I both know that's not how this works.

128.

I WILL TELL YOU THAT KYLA walks out of the woods.

So does Evan.

(He walks straight to a jail cell, and he walks out in hand-cuffs, but still, that motherfucker *walks*.)

His buddy Brandon flies out in a body bag. So does Warden, of course. Hooray, right?

Yeah, well.

So does Lucas.

129.

DAWN'S BACK AT HEADQUARTERS when they bring in the bodies.

She's sitting at a cafeteria table drinking hot tea and eating whatever she damn well feels like—i.e., chicken fingers with ranch dressing—and wearing dry clothes.

(The only spare clothes they had to give her were Polar Bear blue.)

(#MostAdvanced.)

(Dawn figures she's earned it.)

She's sitting there surrounded by concerned and very solici- tous Out of the Wild staff members and counselors, and by a bunch of suits from the head office who are already looking at her like she's a mid-seven-figure lawsuit liability.

Dawn can hear the hushed whispers as the suits study her. As they try to figure out what it'll take to keep her quiet.

She doesn't care about that. Not right now.

Not with the helicopter landing outside.

130.

BRIELLE DOESN'T WALK OFF the mountain. She doesn't fly out in a body bag, either.

Brielle is hurt bad. She's unconscious. The paramedics are saying stuff like *brain swelling* and *blood loss*. As soon as the helicopter off-loads Kyla and Evan and the bodies, it takes off again, this time headed for civilization, a hospital.

Someplace where someone can save Brielle's life.

The paramedics are also saying that if Kyla hadn't stuck around to take care of Brielle, she never would have made it off that ridge. That Kyla gave Brielle first aid as best she was able, kept her stable until help arrived.

Kyla walks off the helicopter amid Brandon's and Lucas's bodies. She follows Evan off the aircraft. Evan is in handcuffs.

Kyla is not.

Kyla finds Dawn where she stands just off the helicopter landing pad. They share a glance with each other, but neither says anything.

Then Kyla walks past and into the Out of the Wild headquarters.

She, too, is swarmed by the counselors.

She, too, is eyed by the suits.

———————

It falls to Dawn to fly out with the next batch of rescuers. A second helicopter, headed for ~~the Raven's Claw~~ Fart Mountain—

(RIP Lucas).

Dawn's the only one who can tell them where Amber fell. She's too tired to explain it and she doesn't know how, anyway. So they give her a helmet and hustle her into the helicopter, and the helicopter takes off and speeds away from headquarters.

It doesn't take long to get over the terrain. What cost the group hours and days takes minutes in the air. Dawn sits at the window and looks out over the forest, the valleys and the ridges. She can see the spur ridge where she and Lucas tried to hide for the night. And she can see the cliff where he died saving her life.

She can pick out every lake and campsite and grueling traverse, and none of it looks as bad from up here as it did down there.

It looks small. Easy.

It looks like nothing.

Fart Mountain, though, still looms. It's still scary. It still makes Dawn shiver, just looking at that bare rock jutting up high from the snow.

She gives the helicopter pilot directions to the backside of the summit, and she can see the ledge where Kyla froze and where Amber fell helping her, and at the base of the ledge she can see a patch of orange jacket sticking out of the snow, and she knows that it must be Christian's body and that Warden must have pushed him off the ledge.

But she doesn't see Amber.

Dawn searches the ground underneath the ledge and doesn't see the counselor, as hard as she looks, and for a moment she thinks she must be mistaken, it must be some other ledge, they're in totally the wrong spot.

But then she sees it, just by straining her eyes: a patch of green hidden in the shadows amid the snowy white northern slope of the mountain. And it's lime green and unnatural and she knows it's Amber's jacket and that Amber is down there.

But the jacket isn't moving.

The helicopter hovers overhead and the green jacket doesn't move, just lies there mostly buried in snow, and Dawn stares out the helicopter window and then she starts to cry, and it's not just for Amber but for Lucas and Alex and Brielle and even Kyla, even Christian a little bit, for Brandon and Evan, too.

And even for Warden.

She's crying because no matter how bad things seemed at the beginning, she'd never in her life imagined this terrible end, all the dying and anger and bloodshed and fear.

She's crying because she wishes she could just go back to last week, when they were all setting out on the trail to Fart Mountain, when all she had to worry about was cooking food and pumping water and dodging angry bears, and maybe choosing between two cute boys.

She's crying because her friends are dead, and her enemies, and because it freaking sucks to have enemies, living or dead.

And now Amber's dead, too.

131.

EXCEPT AMBER ISN'T DEAD.

The helicopter team lowers a rescuer on the end of a wire, and Dawn watches as he approaches the patch of green that is Amber's jacket. And she listens on the radio as he describes what he's seeing.

And at first he's telling the rest of the rescuers that the woman isn't moving, that he sees no signs of life.

But then he pauses, and his voice gets excited.

And when he comes back, he's telling everyone he can feel a pulse.

(Amber's alive.)

And this only makes Dawn cry harder.

132.

DAWN'S MOM AND STEPDAD are waiting for her.

Back at headquarters with a group of other parents who mostly look either angry or sad.

Cam and Wendy look relieved.

They're waiting when Dawn steps off the helicopter, which takes off again immediately to ferry Amber to a hospital.

Cam and Wendy stand close to each other, Cam's arm around Wendy's shoulders like they're the perfect parents, like Cam's always been Wendy's husband and Dawn's dad never existed. They watch Dawn step off the helicopter and look relieved to see her, and Dawn supposes they *are* relieved, but that's not really her concern at the moment.

She skirts Cam as he reaches out for a hug. Goes to Bryce instead, her little brother, who lingers in the background, wide-eyed, looking around as though he had no clue stuff like this actually existed.

Dawn hugs him.

"Don't ever let them kidnap you," she tells him.

Bryce hugs her back. Hard, like he's still a child, like he's as yet unaware that he's a six-foot-plus behemoth who could crush Dawn with one hand.

"Are you okay?" Bryce asks.

Dawn lets him envelop her and she holds on for dear life.

"I am now," she says.

Cam and Wendy are waiting when Bryce lets Dawn go.

Dawn's not ready to speak to them yet.

She skirts Wendy as Wendy reaches for a hug. She crosses the helicopter landing area to the headquarters building, where a gaggle of suits stand in a huddle, still watching her, still adding up the bill they're going to face when this goes to trial.

Dawn picks out the guy with the nicest-looking suit. He's middle-aged and blandly handsome and has black hair going gray.

"I'm not going to sue you," Dawn tells them.

The men blink.

They look at each other.

The man in the nicest suit says, "You're not?"

Dawn shakes her head. "No," she tells him. "Just don't make me go home"—she gestures to Cam and Wendy—"with them."

The men look over her shoulder at Cam and Wendy. The man in the nicest suit clears his throat.

"Ah," he says. "Where would you like to go instead?"

Dawn doesn't hesitate.

"Chicago," she says.

"First class," she says.

Then she turns around and sees Bryce.

"And I want my brother to come, too."

133.

SO THERE YOU HAVE IT.

Dawn goes to Chicago to stay with her nana. Nana is thrilled to see her. Dawn breaks down and cries a little bit, but then she pulls it together. For her nana's sake.

She still cries a lot when Nana can't see her.

Bryce comes, too. He stays for a while and then he goes home again, but Dawn makes him promise not to ever get kidnapped. She makes him promise to call her if he ever needs anything.

Bryce tells her he'll call her. Then he gets in the taxi. Dawn watches him drive away and wonders if she should feel guilty. If she should go back with him.

But she doesn't.

She stays with her nana. She cooks and keeps the house tidy and goes out for groceries, and she and her nana go for walks to the park and play cribbage and watch old movies on Netflix.

She spends her nights on the phone. She's not calling her parents.

She's not calling Julian.

She calls Bryce.

She calls a hospital in Seattle, where Amber is.

Mostly the nurses tell Dawn that the counselor is still unconscious. But they're hopeful she'll be awake soon.

And Dawn FaceTimes with Brielle, who's back home in Oregon. And they talk about how fucked up it all is, what happened on those mountains, and how it's still fucked up now, in the aftermath.

They make plans to meet up somewhere when all the chaos dies down.

"It feels like a bad dream," Brielle says once, and on her phone Dawn can see Brielle's scars, the bruises on her face. "Now that we're home, it kind of feels like it never really happened."

Dawn understands.

She kind of feels the same way.

But it did happen, all of it, and she won't ever forget.

134.

SOMEDAY, DAWN PLANS TO VISIT the graveyard where Lucas is buried. She'll cry at his headstone and thank him for saving her life. She'll tell Lucas's dad how his son was a hero and he would have been great in the army.

But she can't do it yet. Can't face Lucas's parents.

It just hurts too much.

She's not strong enough.

So she keeps calling the hospital where Amber is recovering. She tries to enjoy her time with Nana and forget about what happened out there in the wild.

It's nice, but it just doesn't feel right.

Not quite.

And then one day, Cam and Wendy
show up at Nana's front door.

135.

DAWN'S PARENTS LOOK DIFFERENT, standing there on Nana's porch in Chicago. Wendy looks older than Dawn remembers. Her roots are showing and the crow's-feet around her eyes are deeper.

Cam looks smaller. He looks tired. He has his arm around Wendy and he holds her close, and the two of them look at Dawn standing in Nana's doorway and they seem to nudge closer to each other, and Cam holds Wendy tighter.

And Dawn can see that her mother is scared. And Cam is scared, too.

They're scared of *Dawn*, both of them, and it just feels so . . .

wrong.

136.

DAWN'S FIRST INSTINCT is to hug Wendy, and even Cam.

Her second instinct is to slam the door in their faces.

She does neither.

She stands there and stares at Cam and Wendy, and Cam and Wendy stare back, and neither of them says anything, and Dawn tries to be tough, tries to remind herself that it was Cam and Wendy who had her kidnapped in the first place.

That it was Wendy who replaced her dad, who fell in love with Cam too soon.

That she should hate them both for what they've put her through, for ruining her life even before the kidnapping.

But Cam and Wendy look so old, and tired, and scared.

They look like they've been lost in the forest, too.

And Dawn realizes she can't hate them, as much as she wants to. She realizes, to her horror, that she actually feels kind of *guilty*.

"I'm not going back to Sacramento," she tells them. "Just so you know."

Wendy and Cam glance at each other. "We're not here to

bring you home," Cam tells her. And he squeezes Wendy's shoulder again. "We just want to see for ourselves you're all right."

Beside him, Wendy begins to cry.

And Dawn feels even worse.

137.

THEY CALL AN UNEASY TRUCE, Dawn and Wendy and Cam. They go out for coffee.

They go out for coffee, and as they sit across from each other amid a sea of hurried, stressed-out Chicago people, and sip their drinks, Wendy dabs at her eyes and doesn't say anything, and Dawn watches people go by, and she doesn't say anything, either. And eventually, Cam clears his throat.

"It must have been so scary," he says. "Out in the wilderness."

Dawn sips her coffee and doesn't reply.

And after a long silence, Cam tries again. "We would never have sent you," he says, "if we *knew*, Dawn; they swore to us it was safe."

Dawn still doesn't answer. She knows that he's trying, but she's just not here for it. She doesn't want to give him an inch.

And Cam knows it.

He blows out a breath and drops his head into his hands. And Dawn can see how Cam's lost weight and how skinny he looks and how his whole body shakes when he cries. And she knows he feels guilty, too.

After a few awkward minutes of Cam pretending he isn't crying and Wendy dabbing her eyes and Dawn alternately feeling embarrassed and trying not to cry herself, Cam wipes his eyes with the back of his hand. He looks around the coffee shop and pushes back his chair. "I'm sorry," he says again.

"I'll let you two talk things out," he says.

"I'll just—I'll wait outside."

138.

CAM STANDS.

He puts his hand on Wendy's shoulder and rests it there for a moment, and then he squeezes, and Wendy kind of leans into his hand, without looking at him, and it's a tiny gesture, but Dawn can see how it comforts her mother.

She can see how her mother needs to be comforted.

And then Cam stands up straighter, and he smiles once at Dawn before he turns toward the door, but it's a sad smile, kind of forced, like it actually really hurts him to have to walk away.

To have to leave Wendy when she's in such a state.

And, maybe, to have to leave Dawn.

Dawn thinks about what Brielle said, up on the ridge, about how Dawn didn't wind up in Out of the Wild because her dad died, or because Wendy met Cam. She thinks about how stupid she felt when she told Brielle her reasons and Brielle shot them down.

You're here because you don't know how to cope, Brielle said.

Because you chose drugs and some asshole named Julian instead of dealing with your feelings like an adult.

Dawn misses her dad. But that's not Cam's fault.

It's not Wendy's fault she found someone new.

Dawn knows this now, and maybe she always did. Maybe she's just finally sick of pretending she doesn't.

And Dawn tells herself this doesn't mean anything, not yet. It doesn't mean she has to listen to him, or that he's replacing her father.

It doesn't mean she has to go home to Sacramento.

(It doesn't even mean she has to *like* Cam yet.)

She isn't sure where they all go from here, and she's not dumb enough to think all her problems are solved.

(They're not.)

She's not even sure she'll be okay, not yet.

But Wendy sets down her Kleenex and reaches across the table and takes Dawn's hand in her own, and it's warm and familiar and good and comforting.

And Dawn doesn't feel so alone, for once, and maybe that's enough for now.

Cam's at the door to the coffee shop, waiting to leave as some hipsters barge in. And Dawn takes a deep breath and calls his name as he's standing there.

"Cam," she says. "Come back. You can stay."

ACKNOWLEDGMENTS

First of all, shouts to my agent, Stacia Decker, and my editor, Wendy Loggia, and to all of the wonderful people at Delacorte Press who helped shepherd this book from a dream into reality.

Thanks to Jason Parent and Darren Morneau for being there when I climbed my own personal Raven's Claw, and for being ready to run back to headquarters for help when it all went south.

Thanks to Cam and Wendy M. for being lovely, and to Kyla Dawn for the inspiration.

And finally, thanks to my family—Mom, Dad, Andrew, Terry, Laura, and Little E—for being the raddest in every possible way.

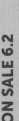